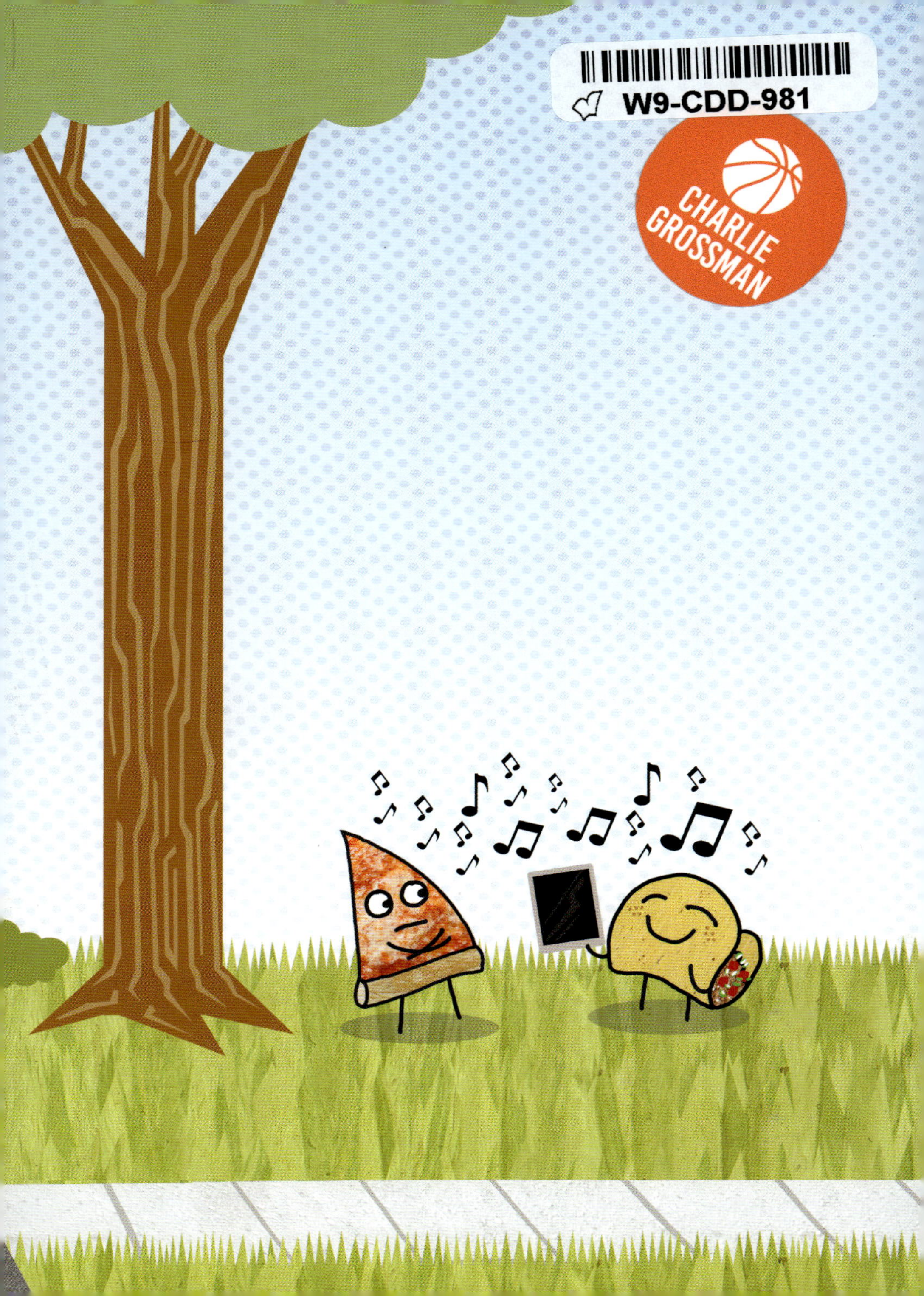
CHARLIE
GROSSMAN

You know you want to read
ALL the Pizza and Taco books!

WHO'S THE BEST?

BEST PARTY EVER!

SUPER-AWESOME COMIC!

TOO COOL FOR SCHOOL

ROCK OUT!

DARE TO BE SCARED!
(Coming in July 2023)

Pizza and Taco

ROCK OUT!

STEPHEN SHASKAN

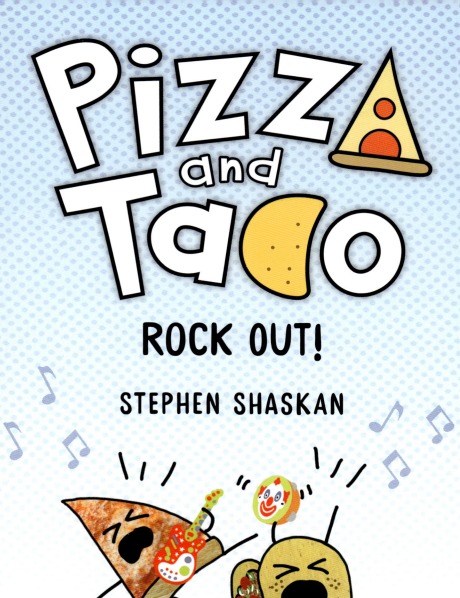

A STEPPING STONE BOOK™

Random House New York

For Rich, Jim, and Nate!
Rock on!

Copyright © 2023 by Stephen Shaskan
All rights reserved. Published in the United States by Random House Children's Books,
a division of Penguin Random House LLC, New York.
Random House and the colophon are registered trademarks and RH Graphic with
the book design is a trademark of Penguin Random House LLC.
Visit us on the Web! rhcbooks.com
Educators and librarians, for a variety of teaching tools, visit us at RHTeachersLibrarians.com

Library of Congress Cataloging-in-Publication Data is available upon request.
ISBN 978-0-593-48124-0 (trade) — ISBN 978-0-593-48125-7 (lib. bdg.) —
ISBN 978-0-593-48126-4 (ebook)

MANUFACTURED IN CHINA
10 9 8 7 6 5 4 3
First Edition

Contents

Chapter 1

Let's Be a Band!

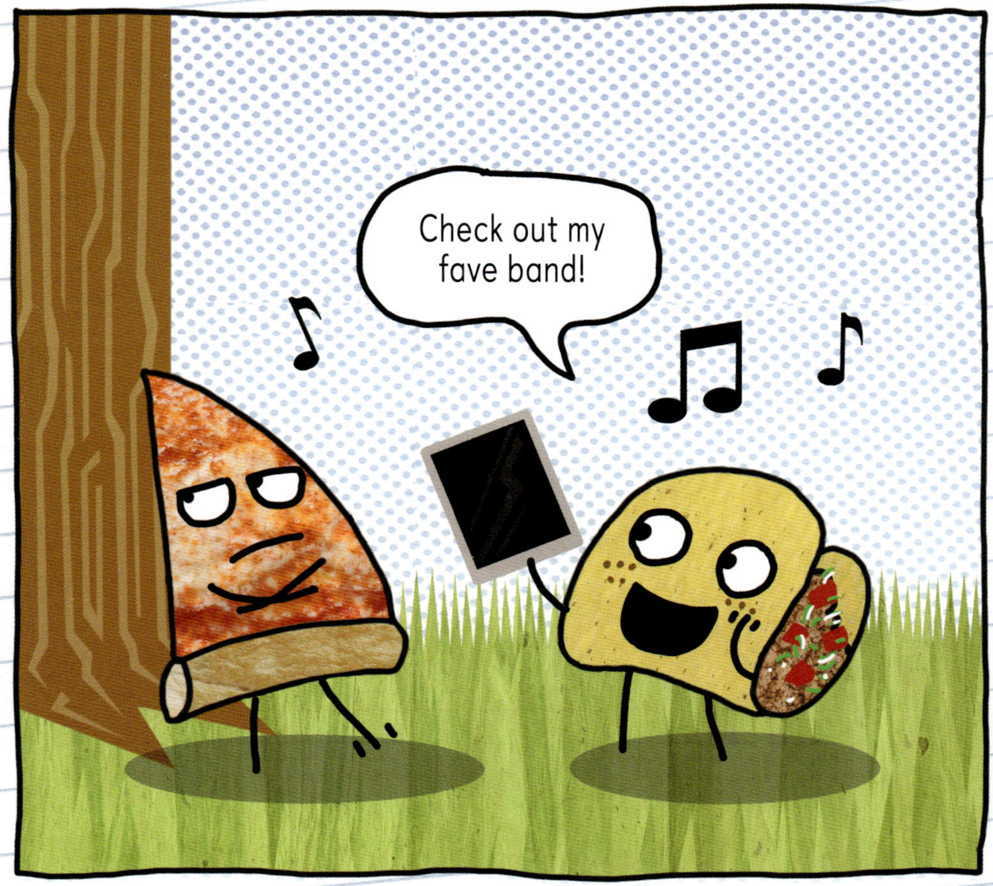

Check out my fave band!

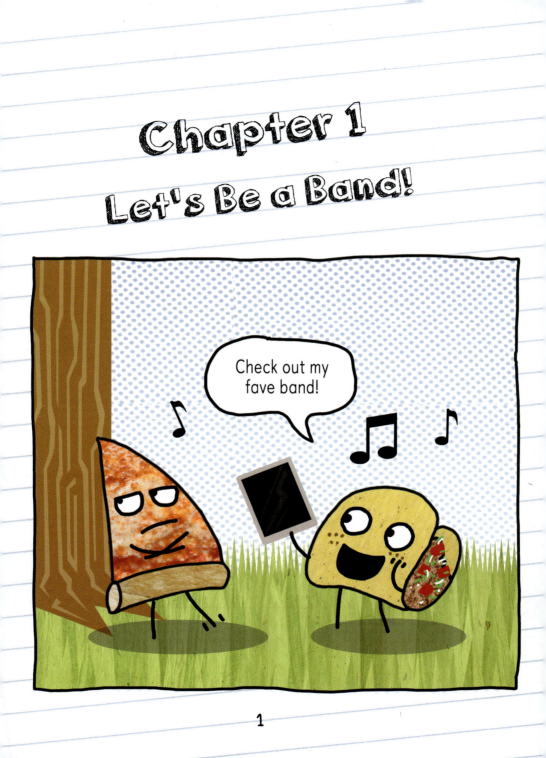

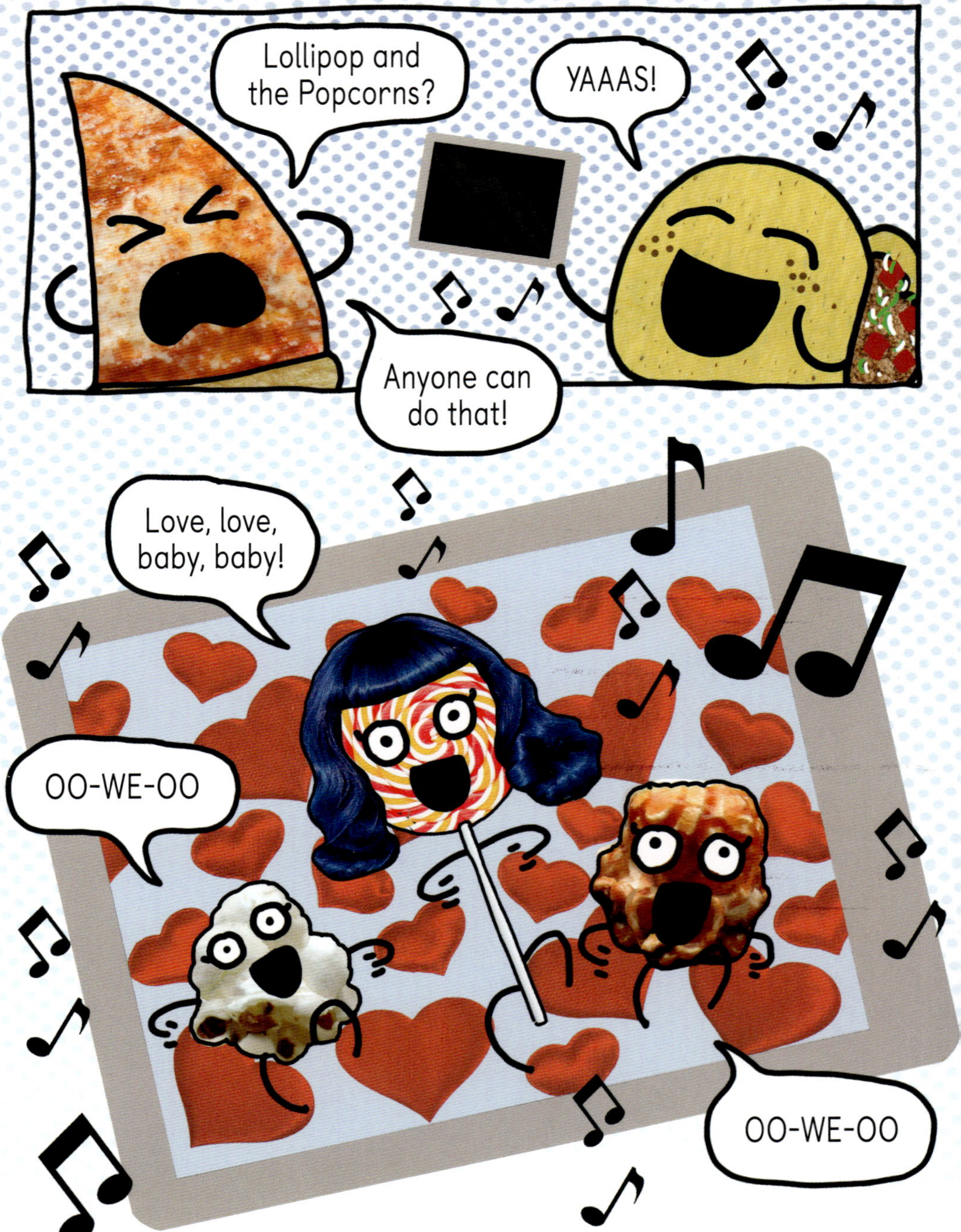
Lollipop and the Popcorns?
YAAAS!
Anyone can do that!
Love, love, baby, baby!
OO-WE-OO
OO-WE-OO

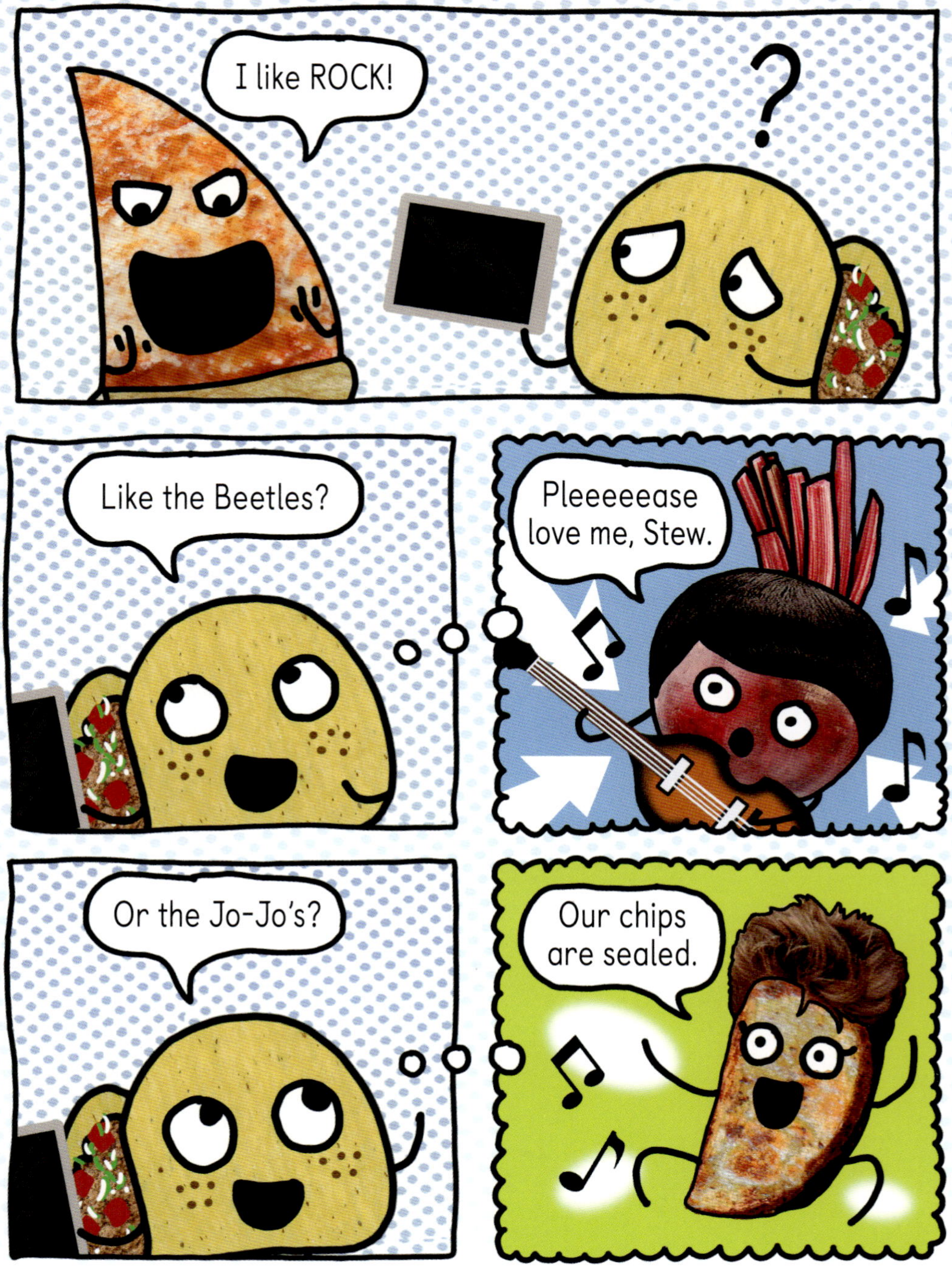
I like ROCK!
?
Like the Beetles?
Pleeeeease love me, Stew.
Or the Jo-Jo's?
Our chips are sealed.

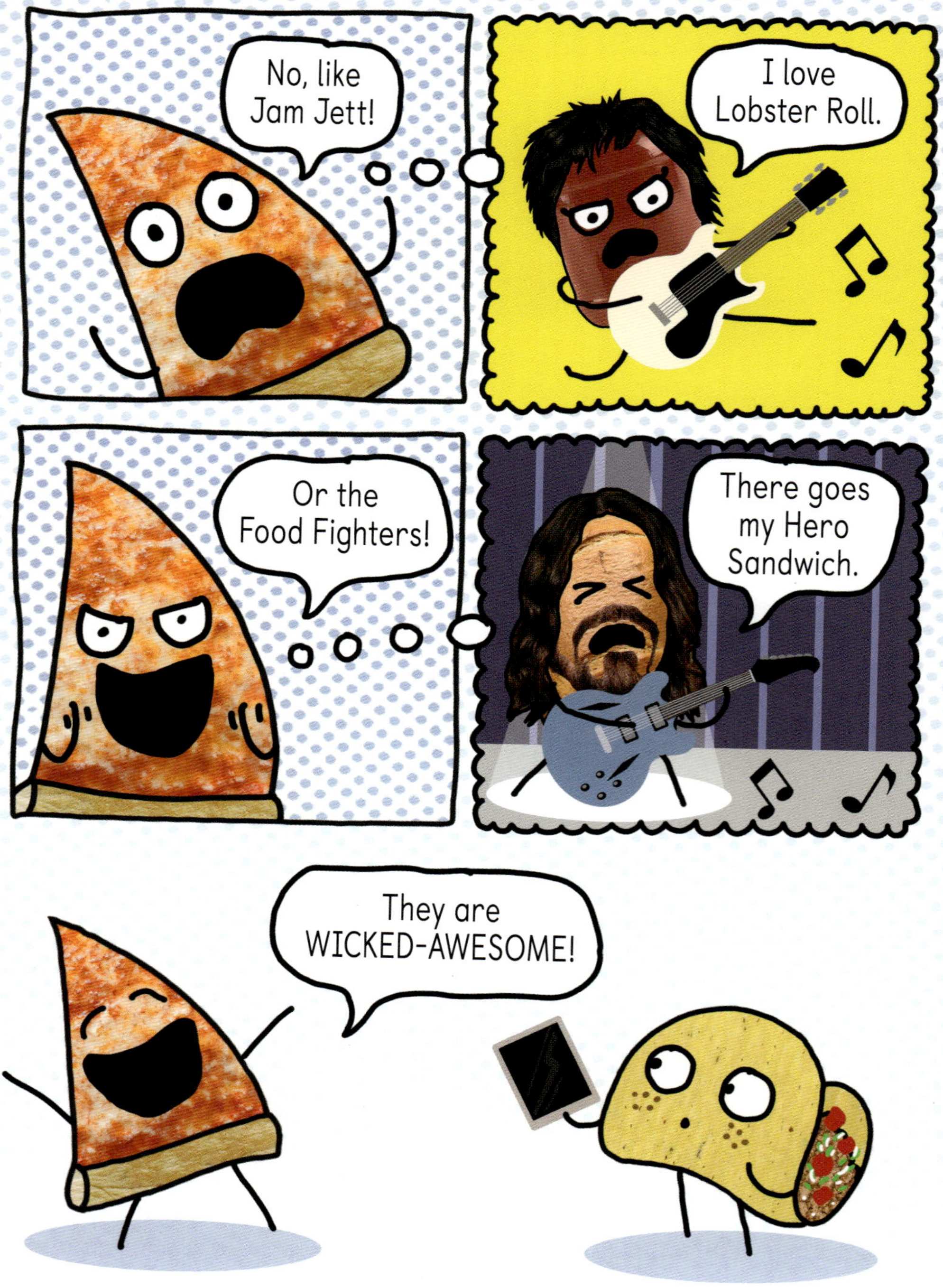

No, like Jam Jett!
I love Lobster Roll.
Or the Food Fighters!
There goes my Hero Sandwich.
They are WICKED-AWESOME!

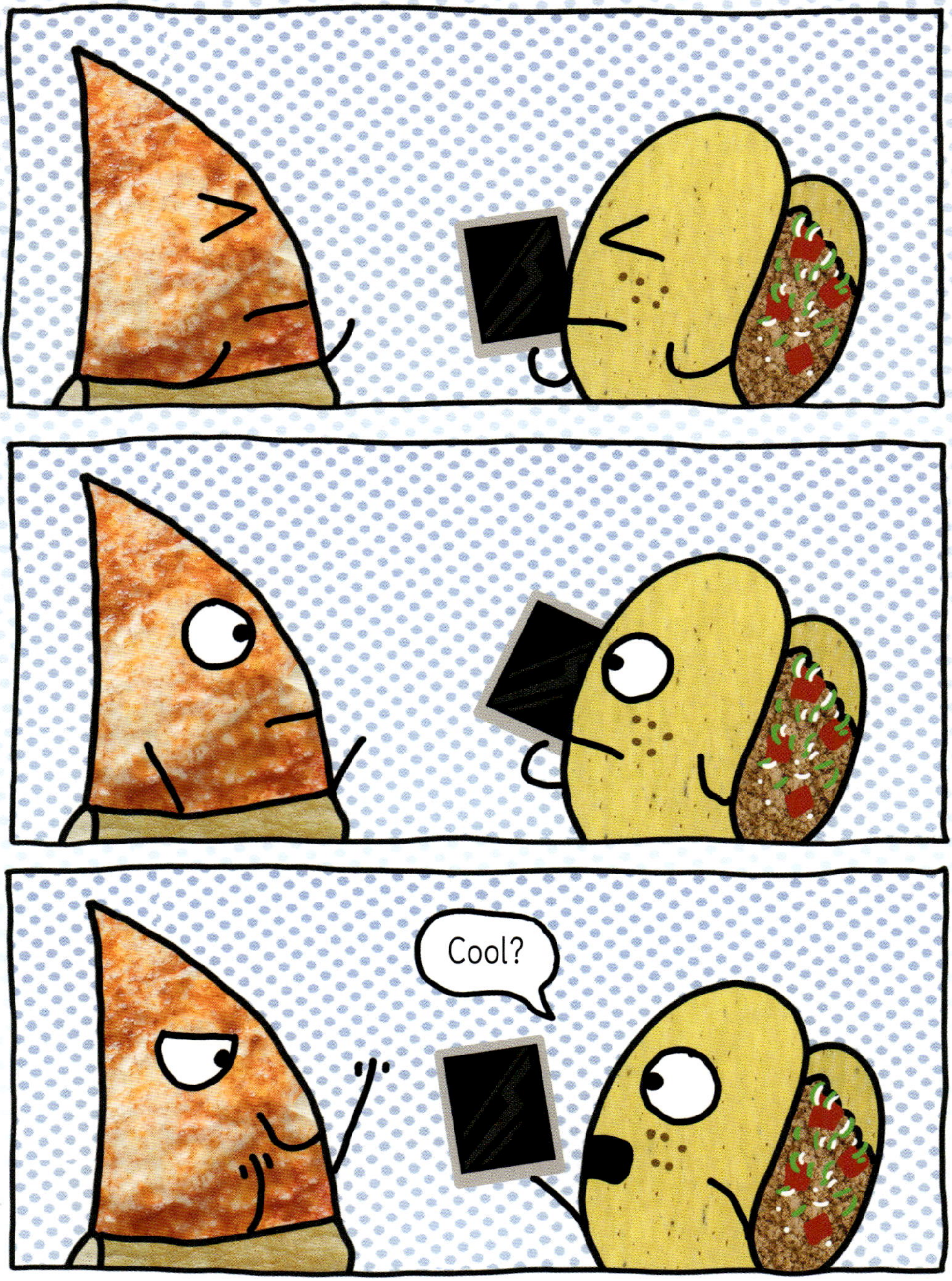
Cool?

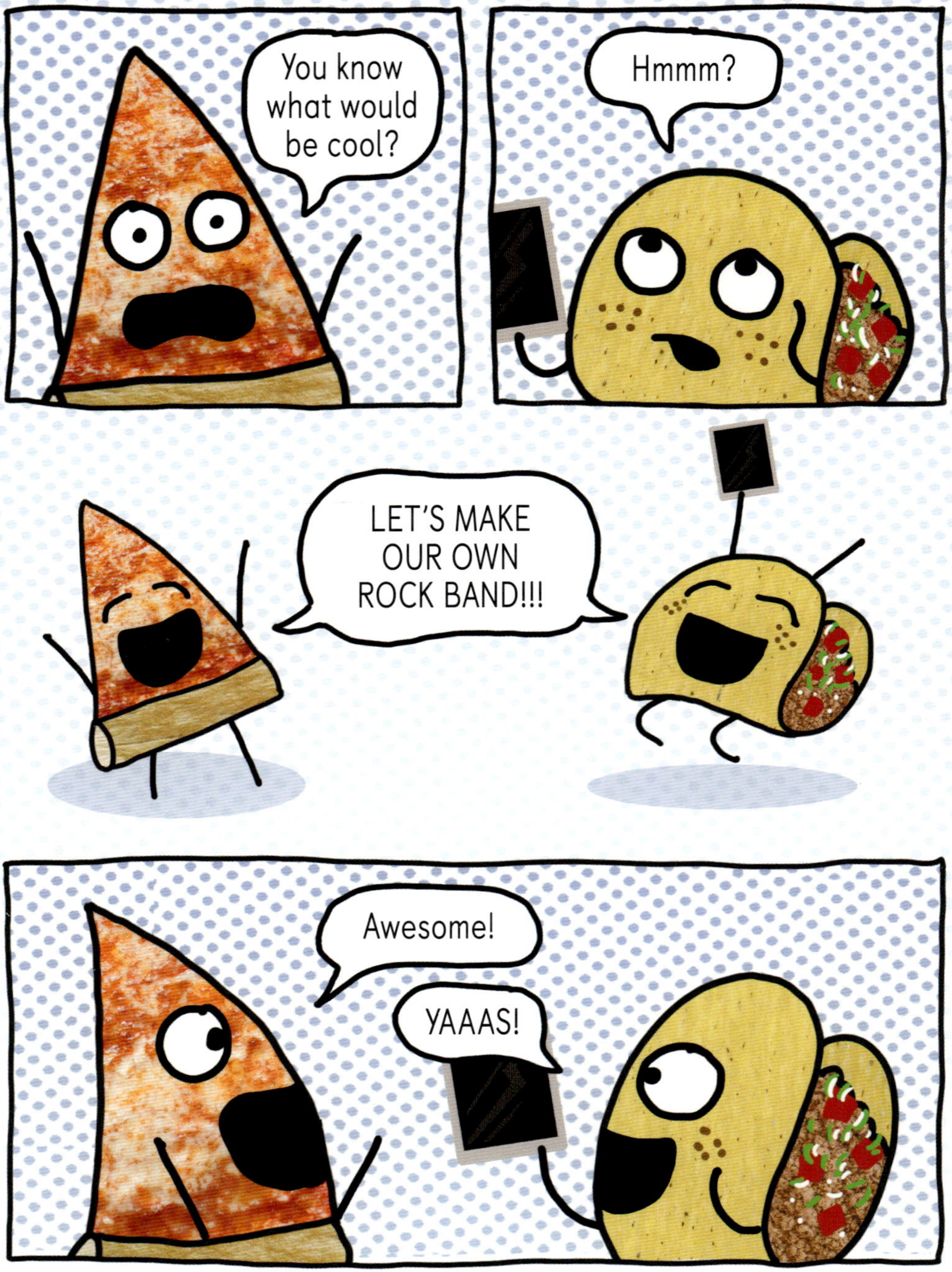
You know what would be cool?
Hmmm?
LET'S MAKE OUR OWN ROCK BAND!!!
Awesome!
YAAAS!

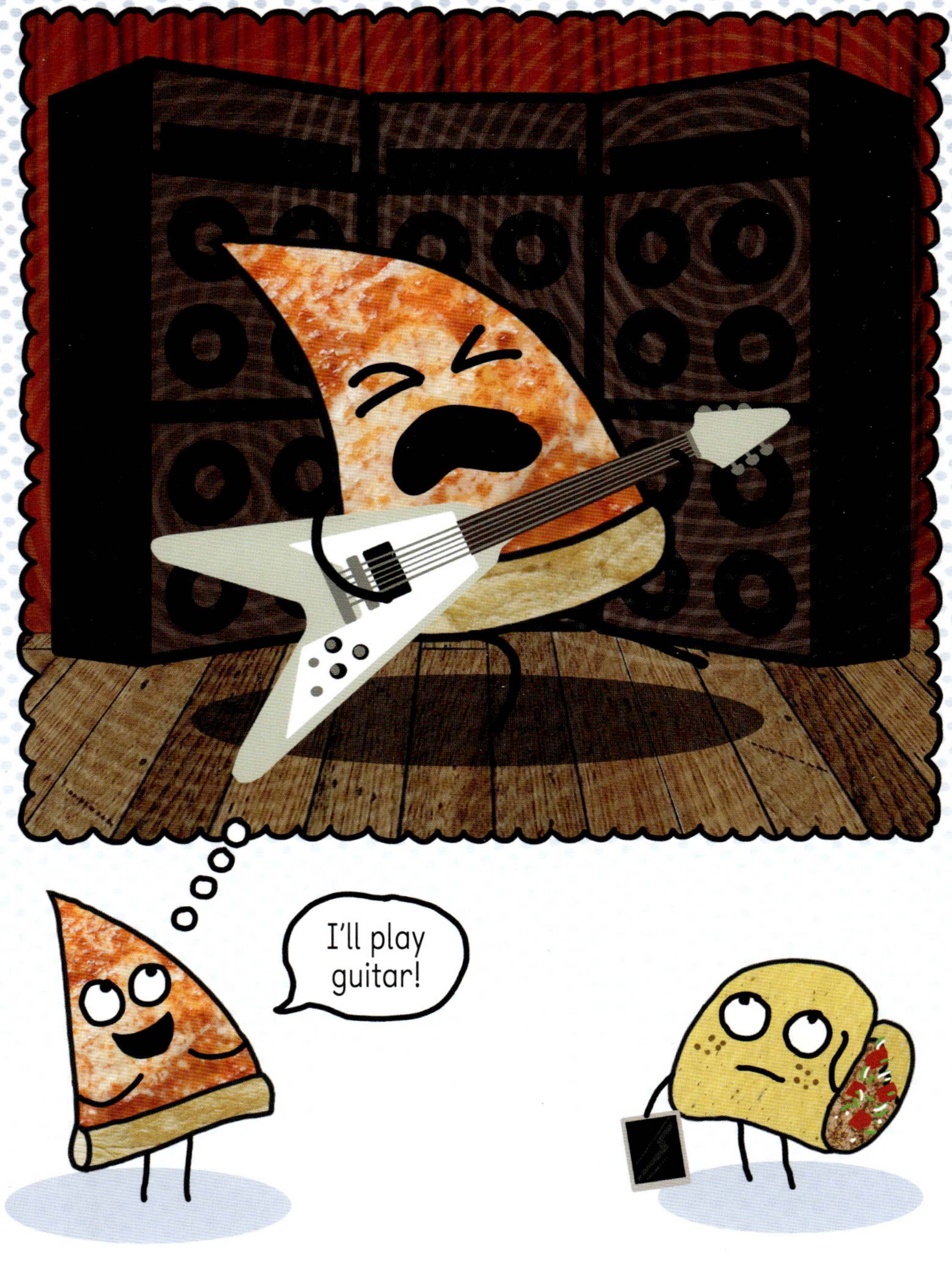
I'll play guitar!

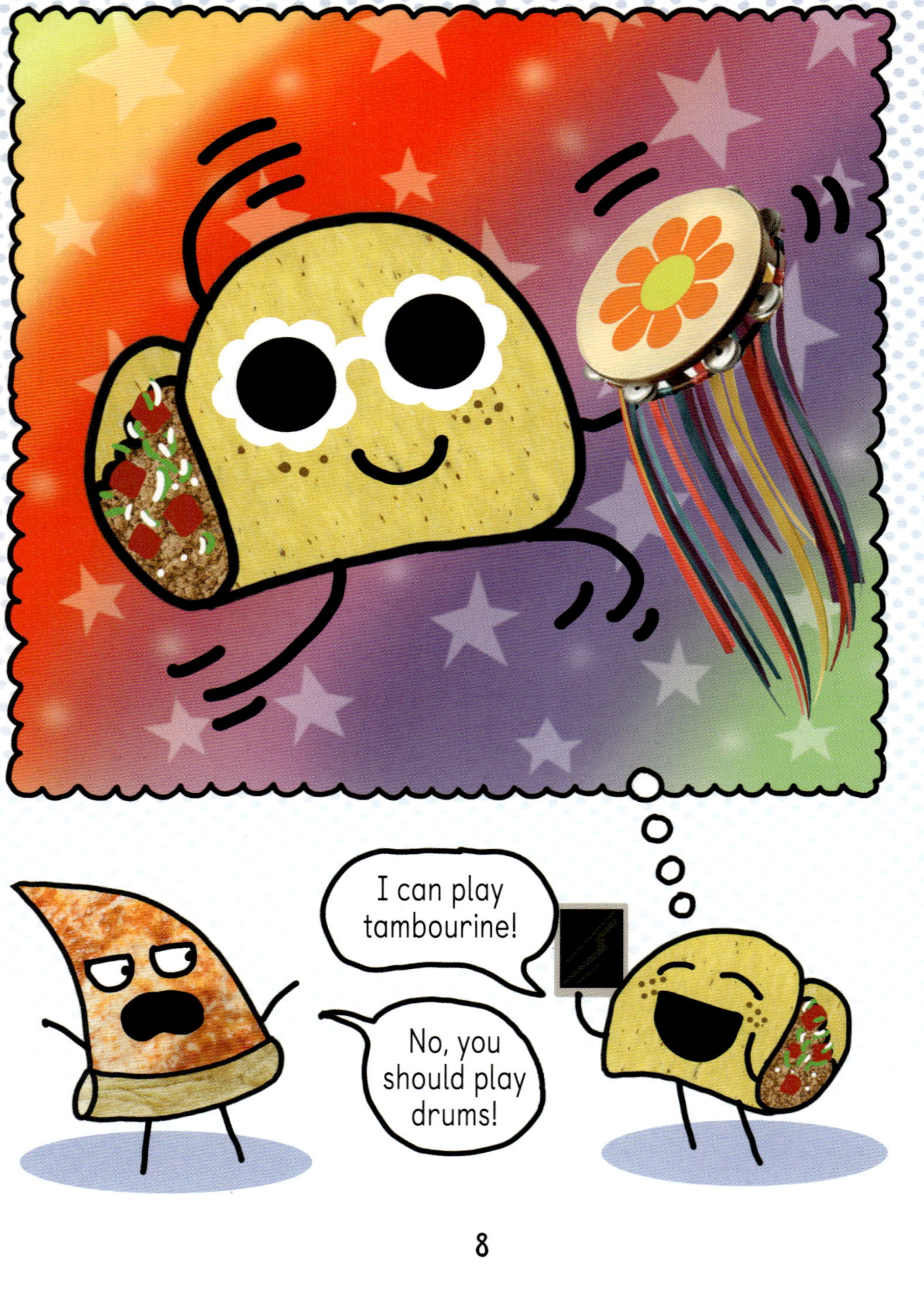
I can play tambourine!
No, you should play drums!

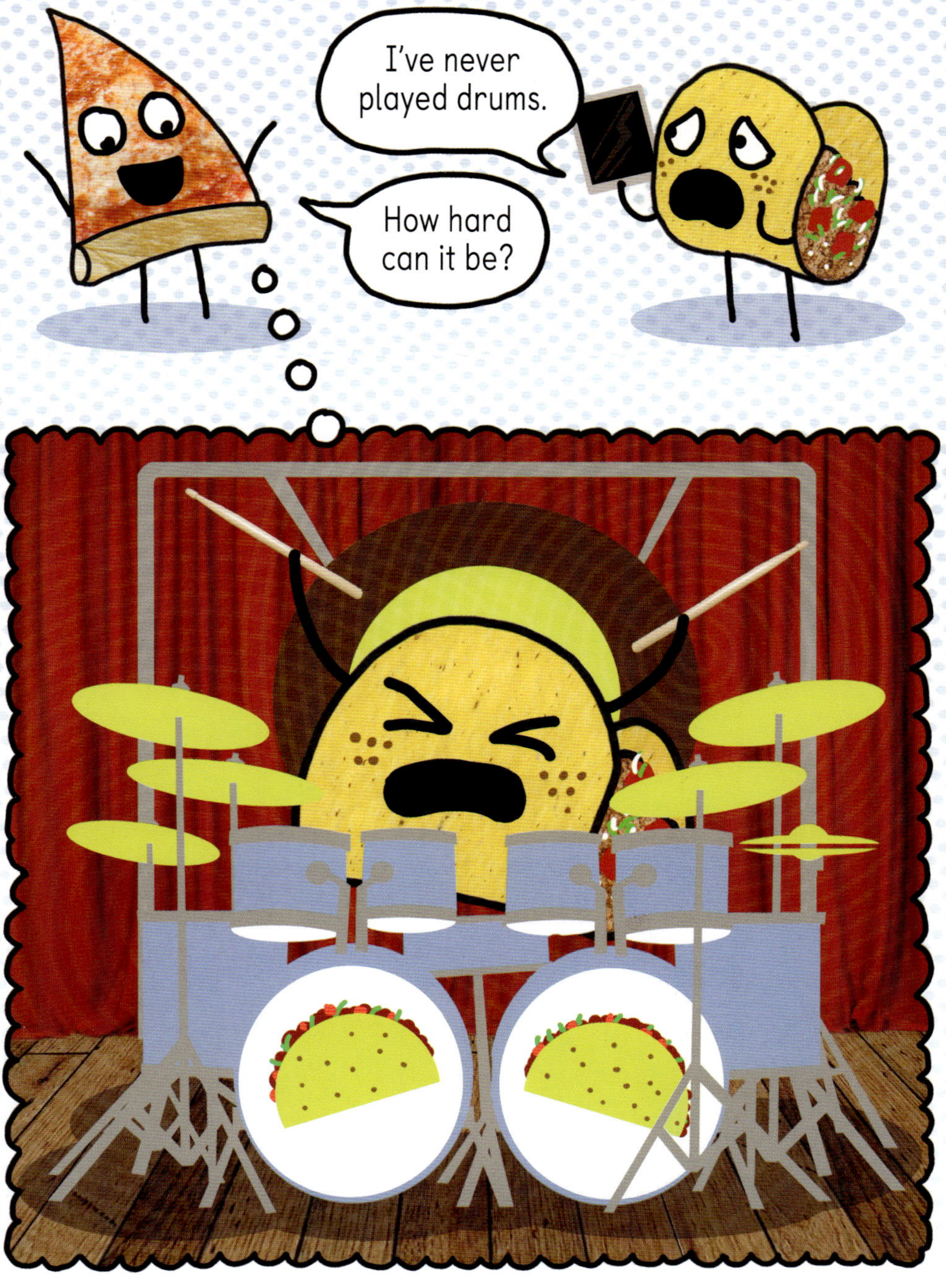
I've never played drums.
How hard can it be?

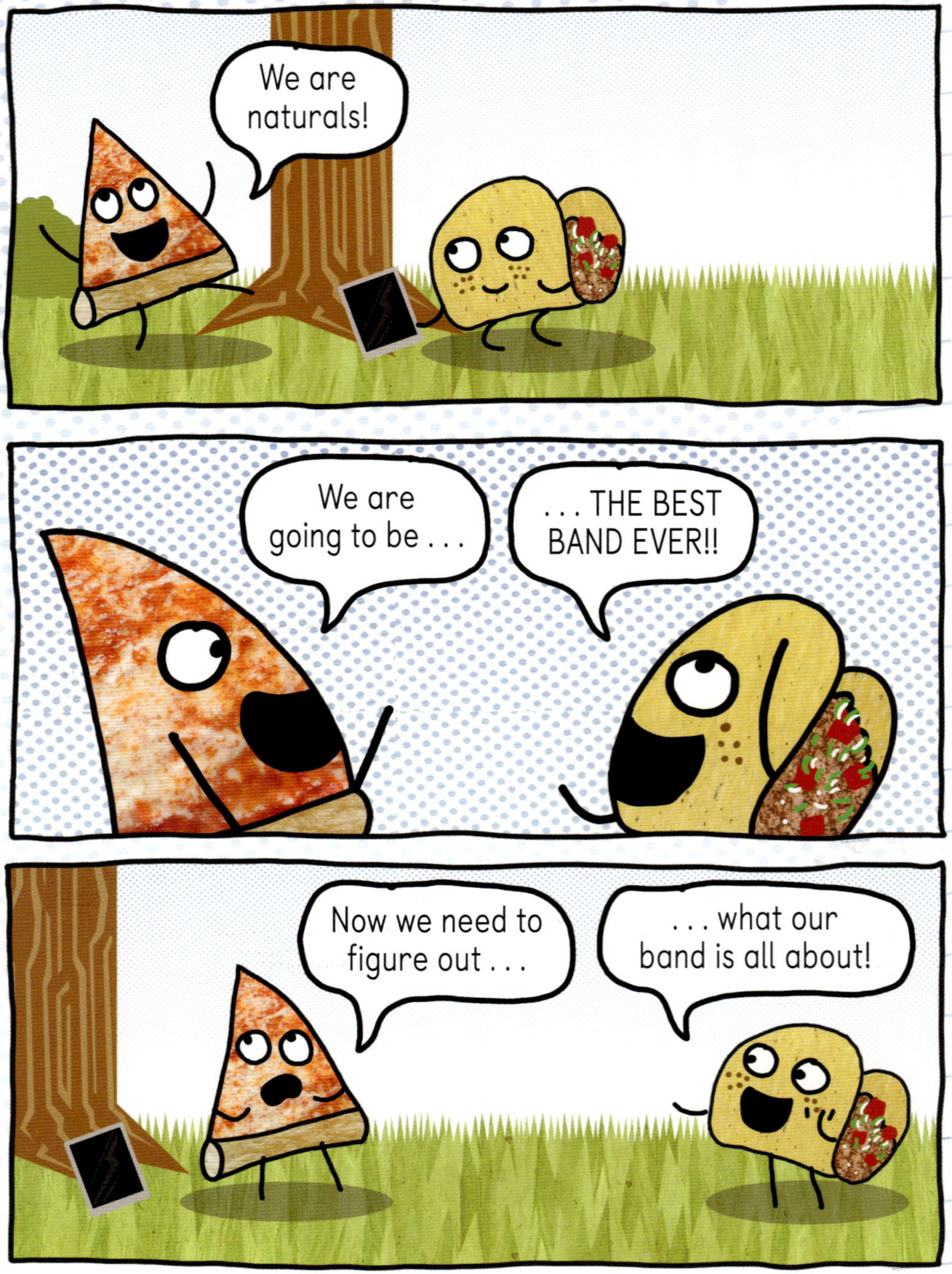
We are naturals!
We are going to be . . .
. . . THE BEST BAND EVER!!
Now we need to figure out . . .
. . . what our band is all about!

Chapter 2
Pizza and Taco's Band

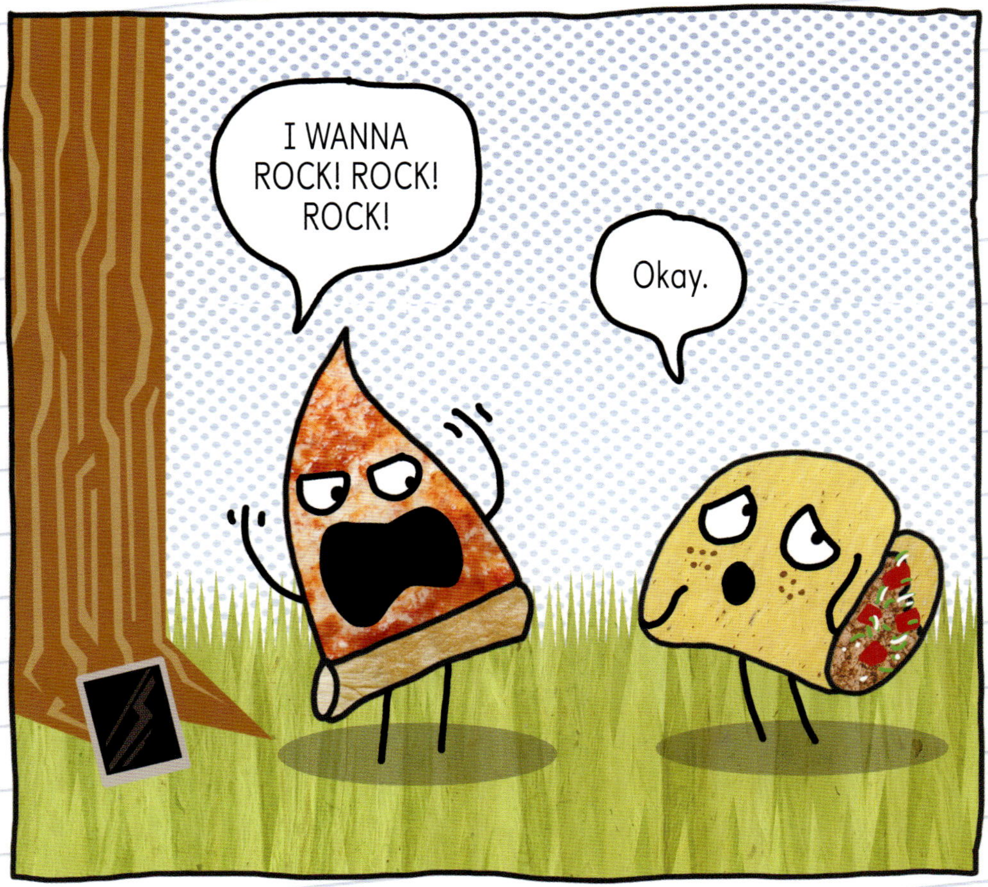
I WANNA ROCK! ROCK! ROCK!
Okay.

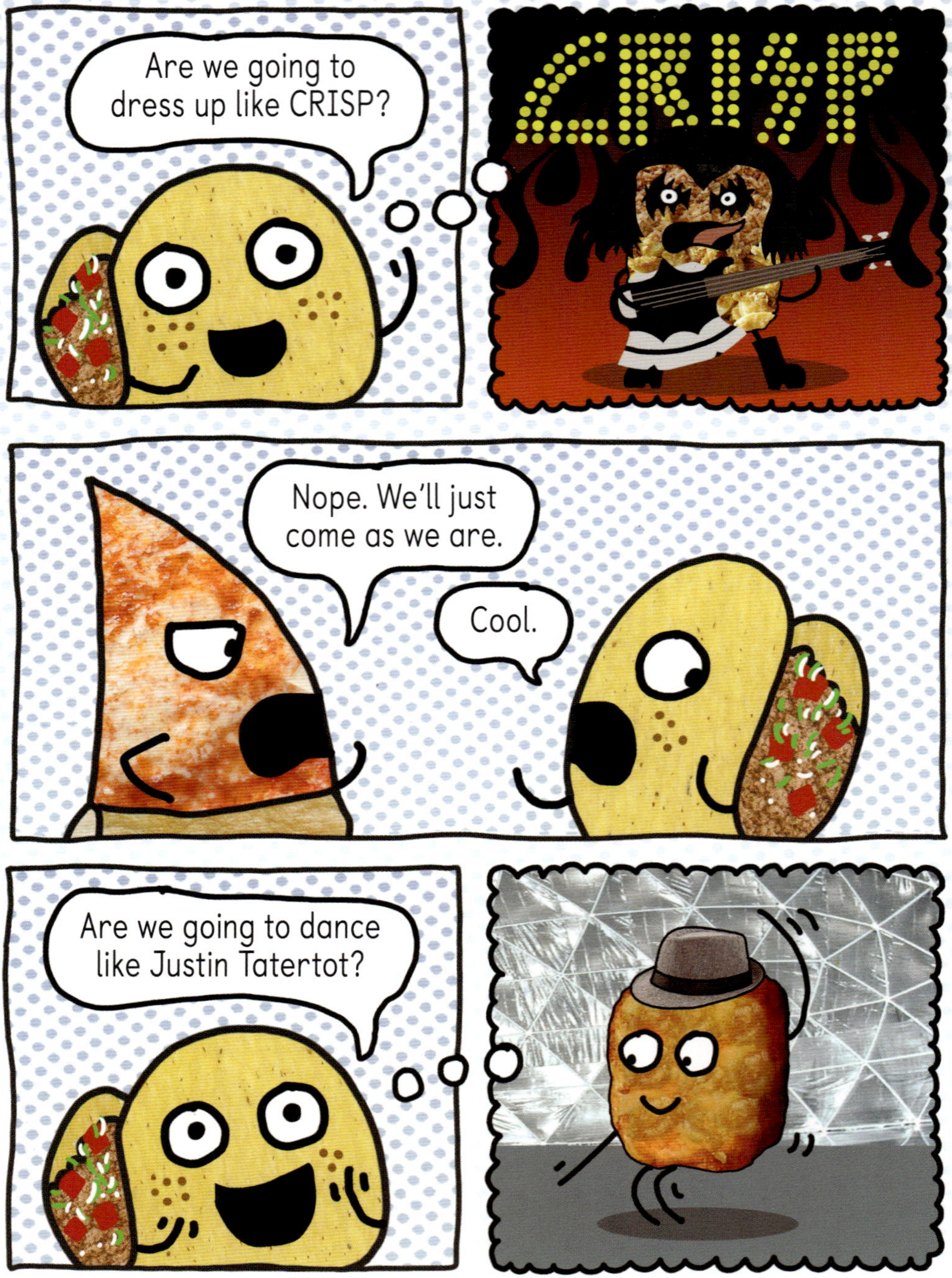
Are we going to dress up like CRISP?
CRISP
Nope. We'll just come as we are.
Cool.
Are we going to dance like Justin Tatertot?

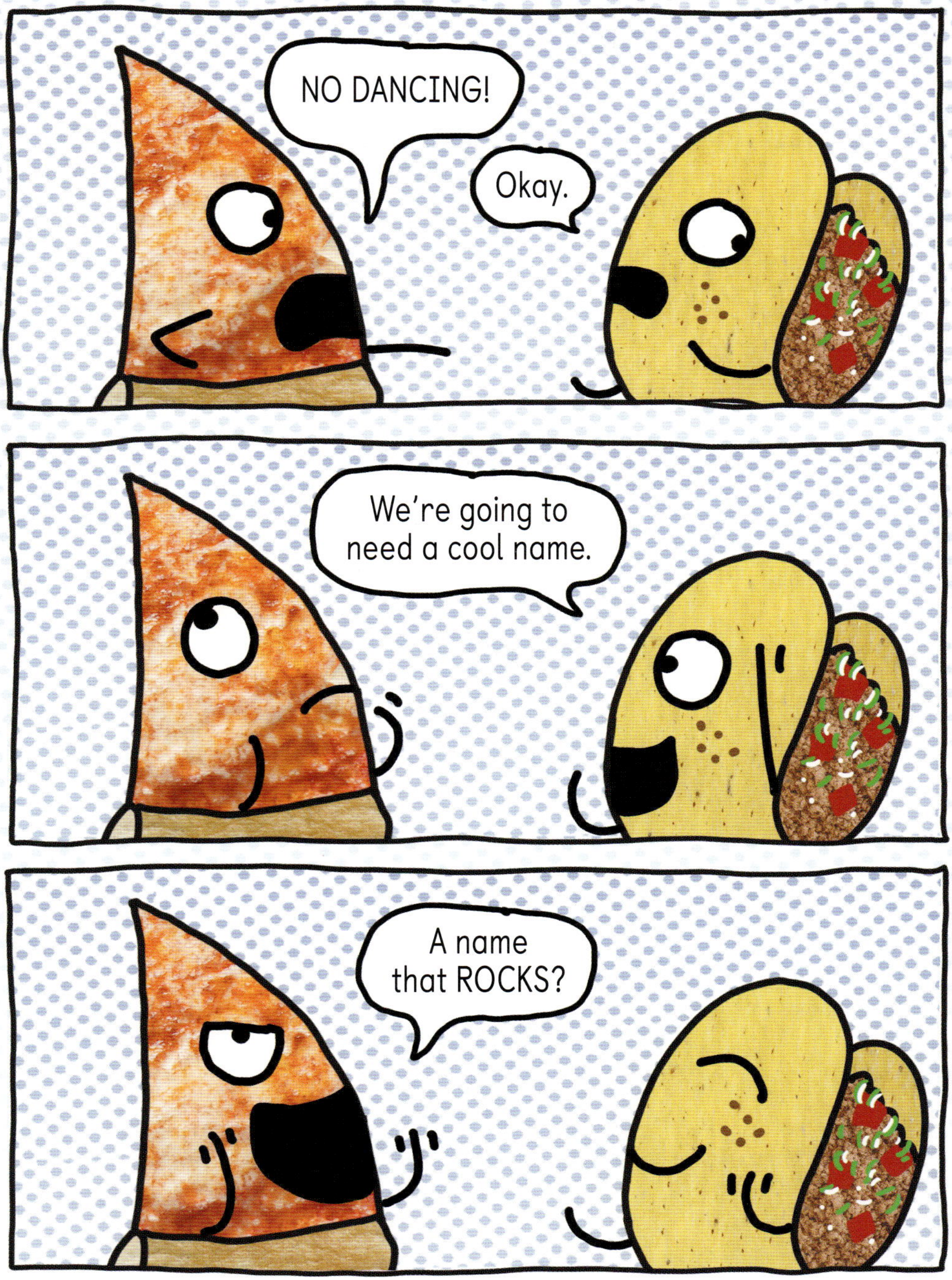
NO DANCING!
Okay.
We're going to need a cool name.
A name that ROCKS?

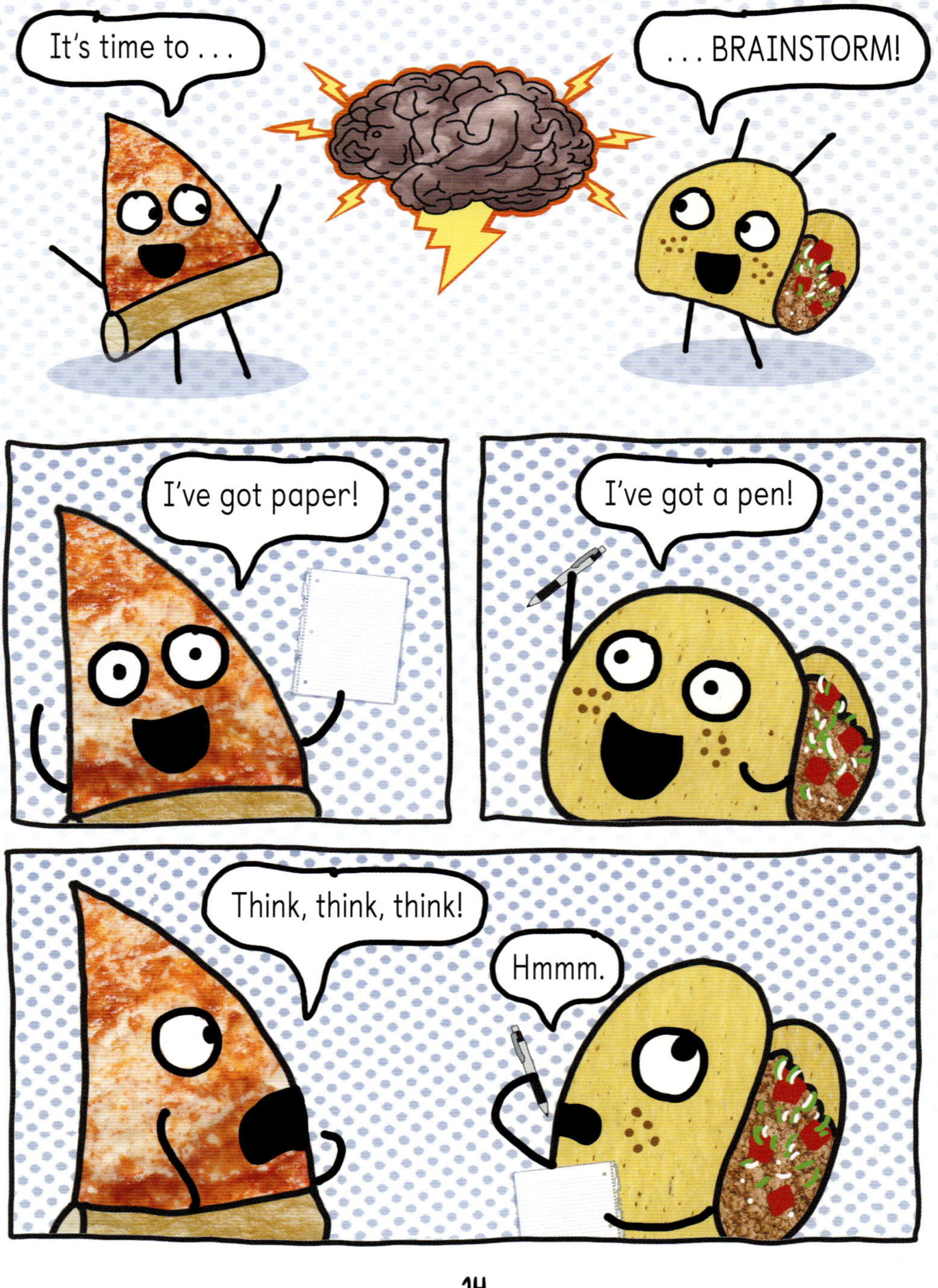
It's time to . . .
. . . BRAINSTORM!
I've got paper!
I've got a pen!
Think, think, think!
Hmmm.

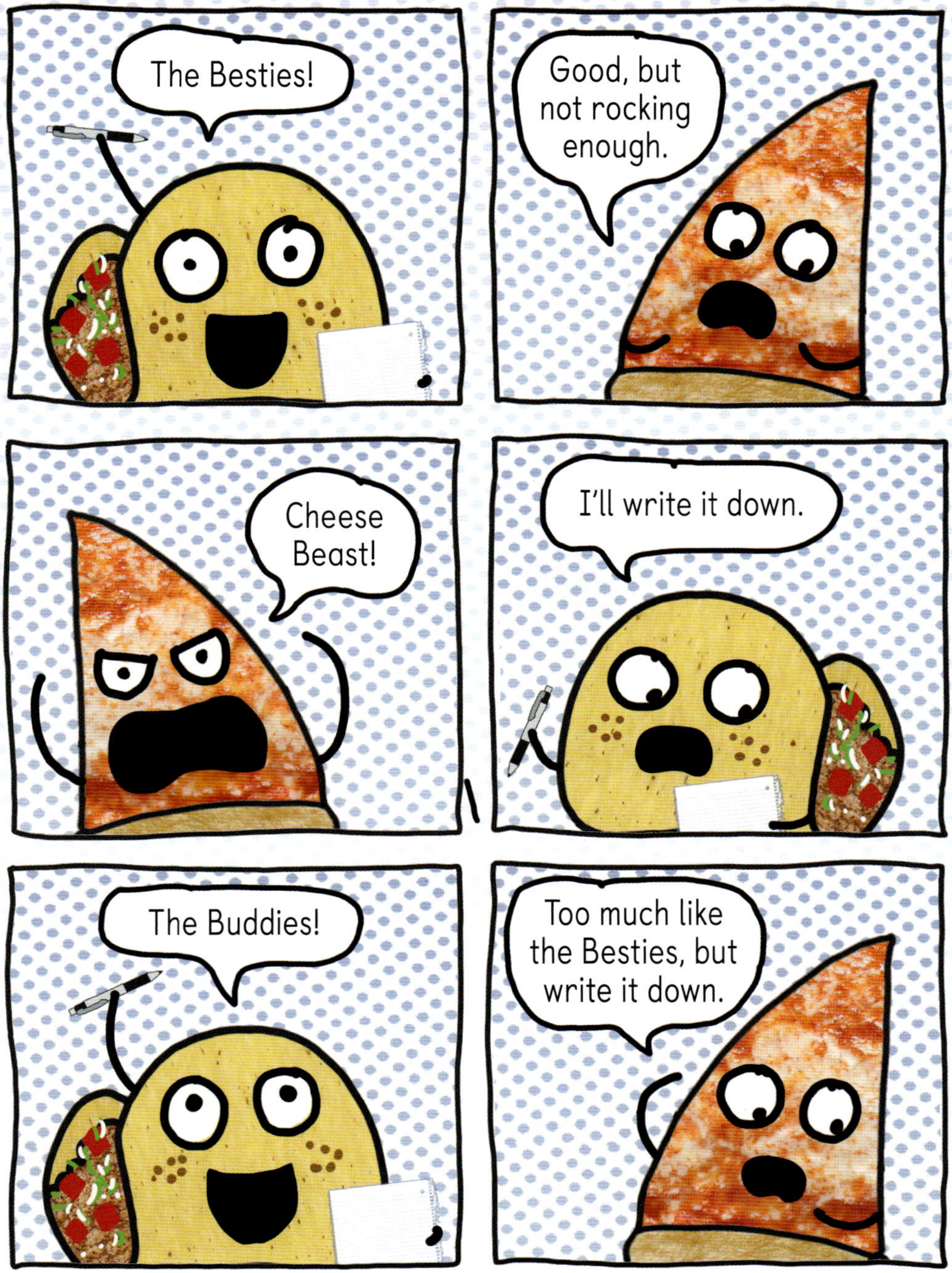
The Besties!
Good, but not rocking enough.
Cheese Beast!
I'll write it down.
The Buddies!
Too much like the Besties, but write it down.

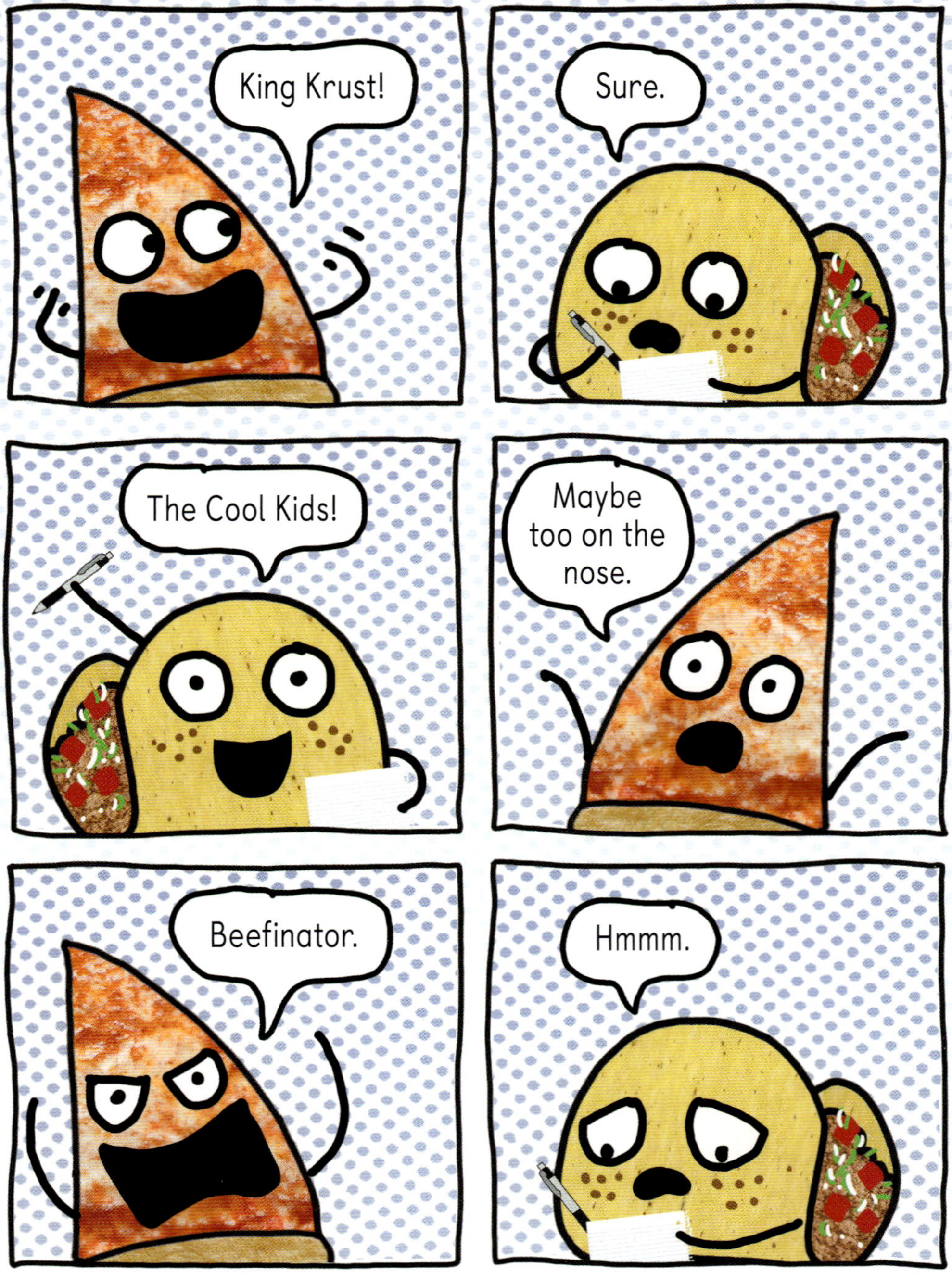
King Krust!
Sure.
The Cool Kids!
Maybe too on the nose.
Beefinator.
Hmmm.

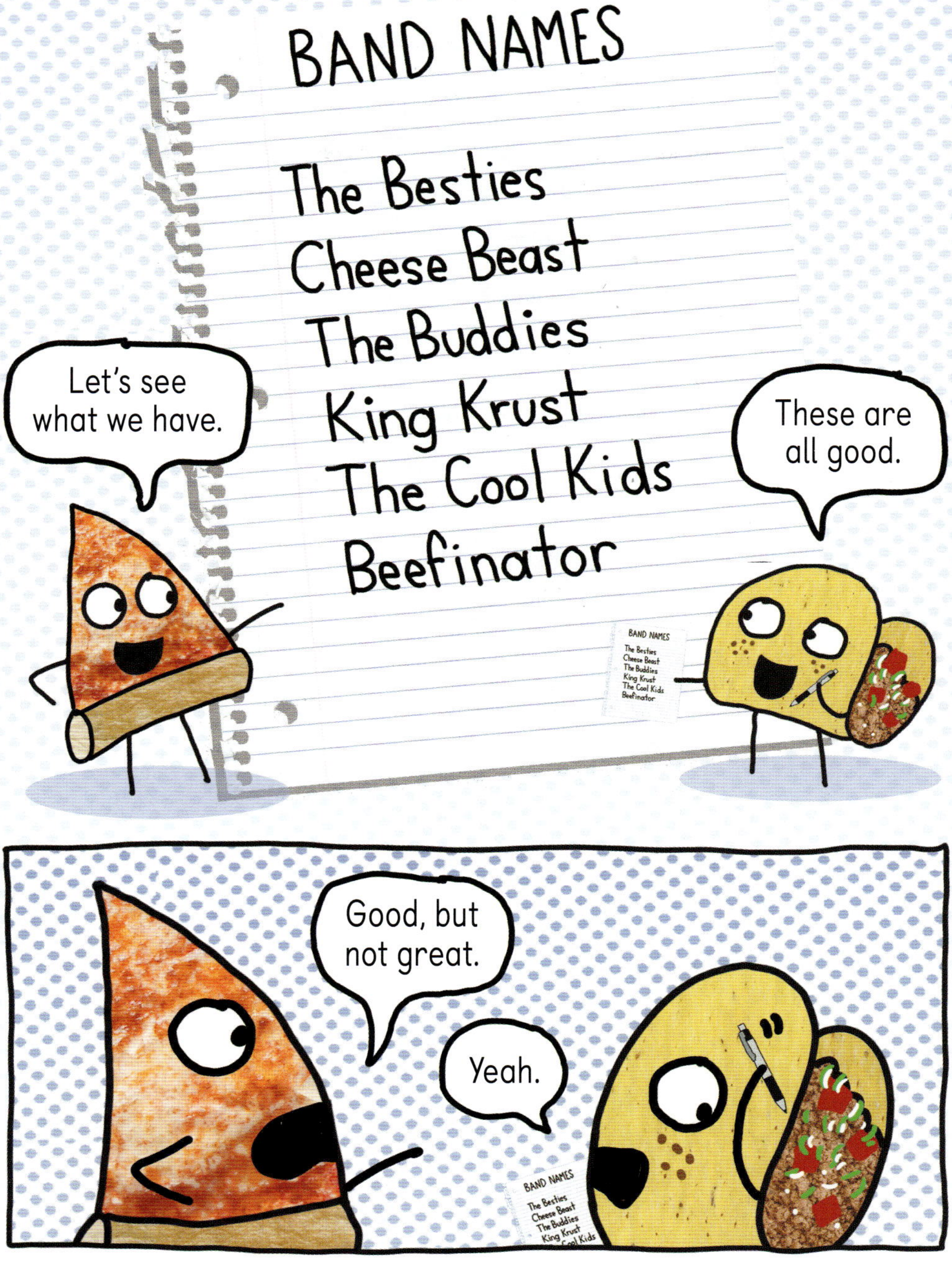
BAND NAMES
The Besties
Cheese Beast
The Buddies
King Krust
The Cool Kids
Beefinator
Let's see what we have.
These are all good.
Good, but not great.
Yeah.

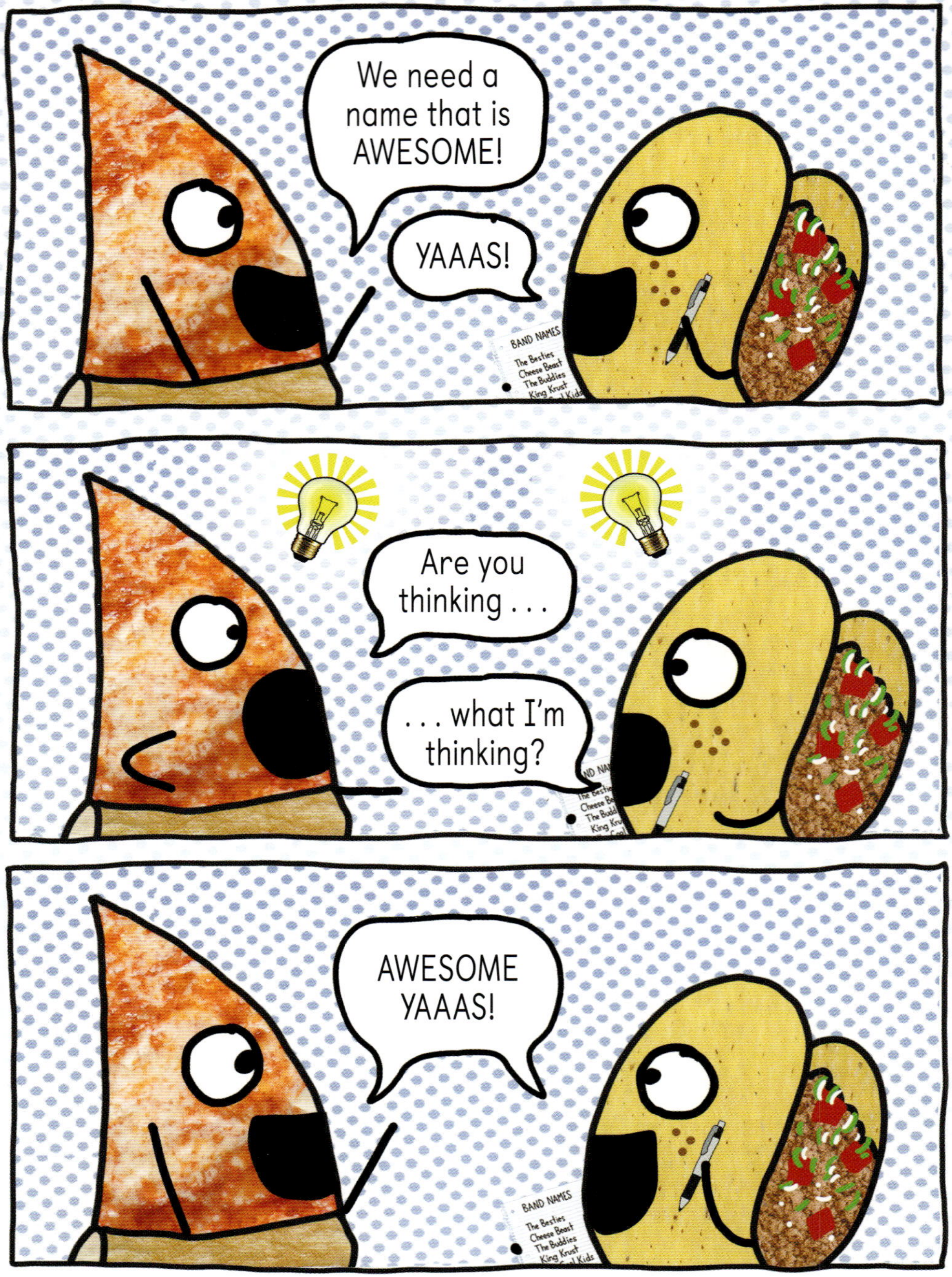
We need a name that is AWESOME!
YAAAS!
BAND NAMES
The Besties
Cheese Beast
The Buddies
King Krust
Are you thinking . . .
. . . what I'm thinking?
AWESOME YAAAS!
BAND NAMES
The Besties
Cheese Beast
The Buddies
King Krust

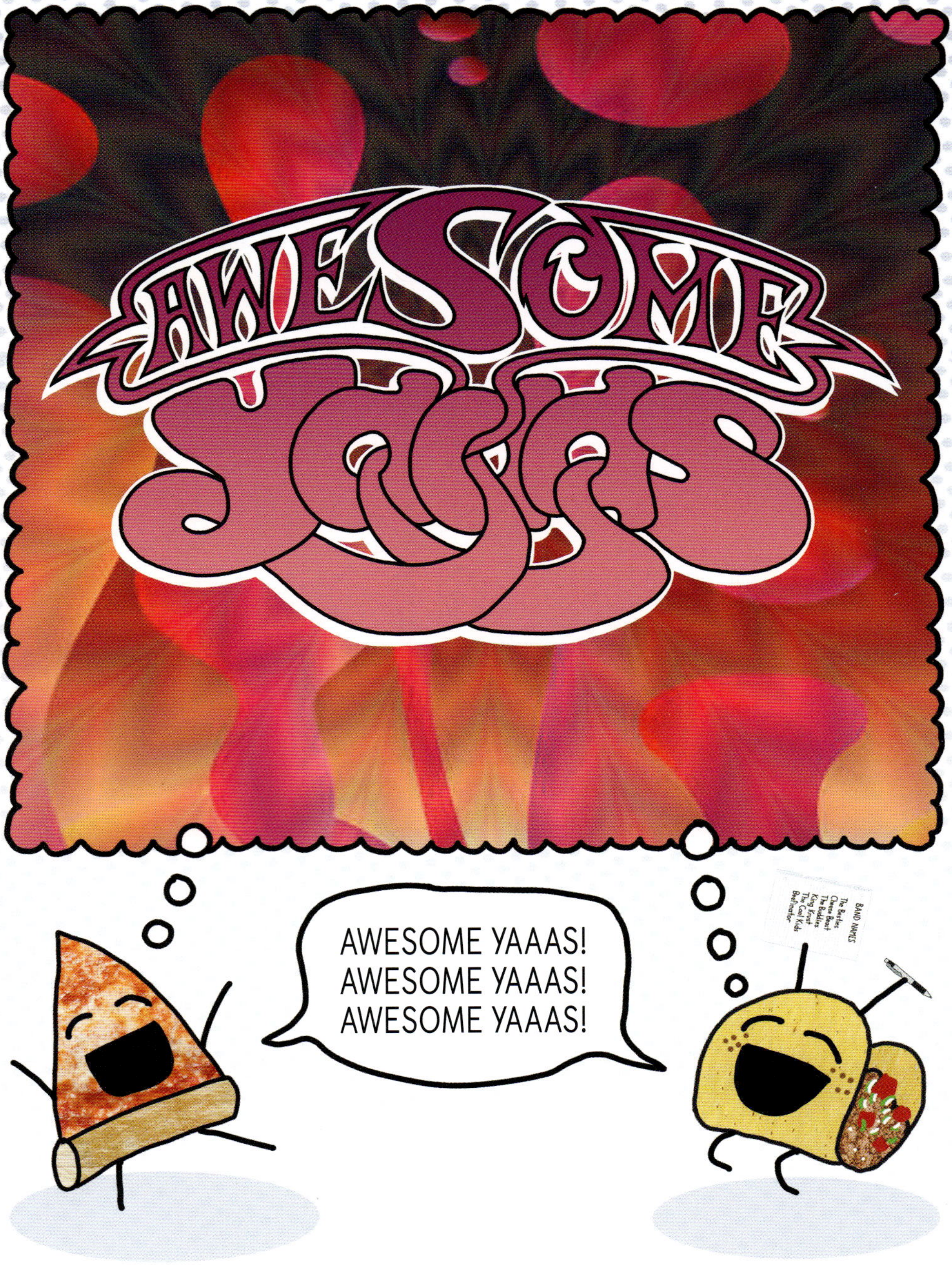
AWESOME YAAAS
AWESOME YAAAS!
AWESOME YAAAS!
AWESOME YAAAS!
BAND NAMES
The Besties
Cheese Beast
The Buddies
King Krust
The Cool Kids
Beefinator

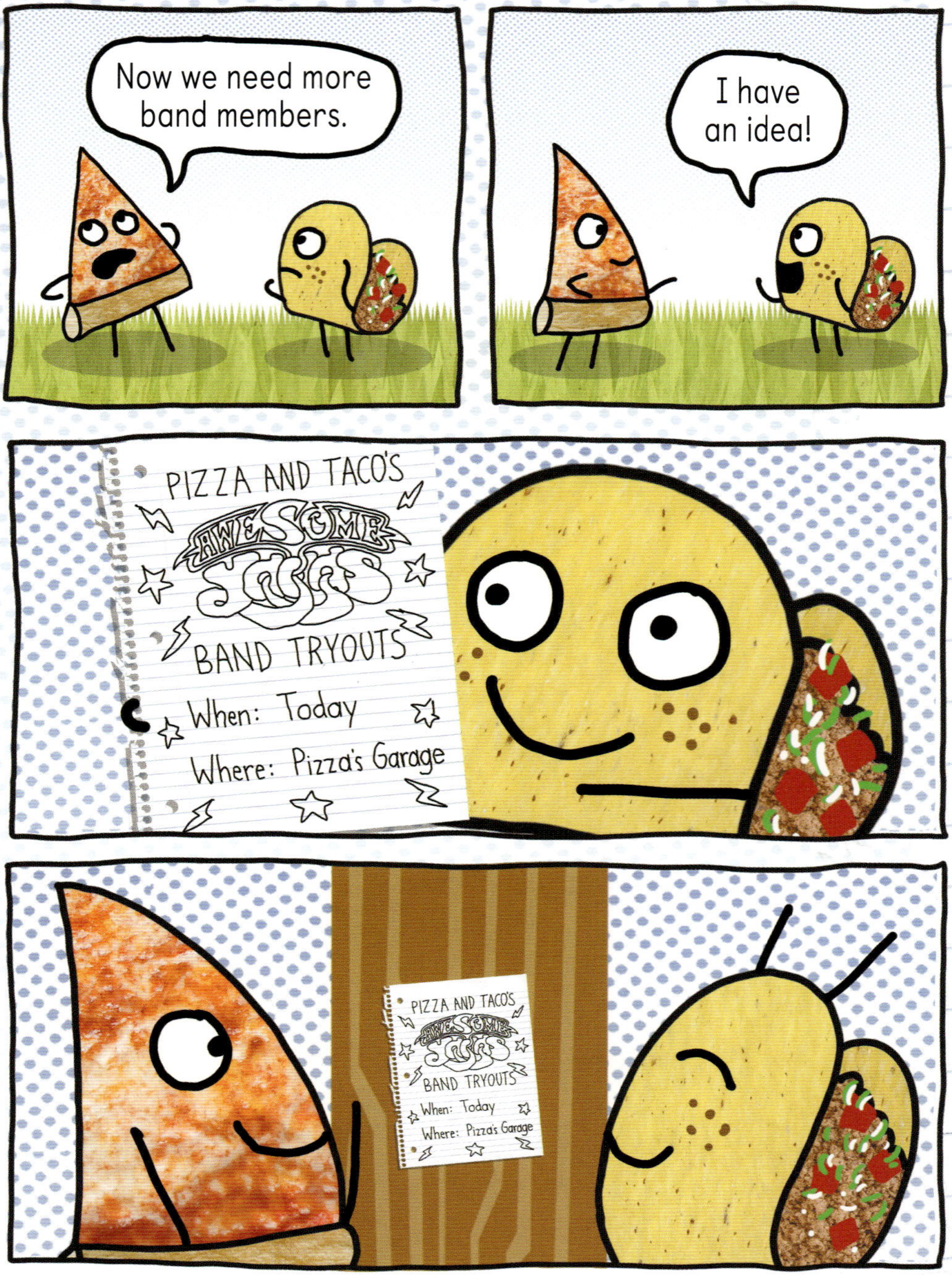
Now we need more band members.
I have an idea!
PIZZA AND TACO'S
AWESOME
BAND TRYOUTS
When: Today
Where: Pizza's Garage
PIZZA AND TACO'S
AWESOME
BAND TRYOUTS
When: Today
Where: Pizza's Garage

Chapter 3
Band Tryouts

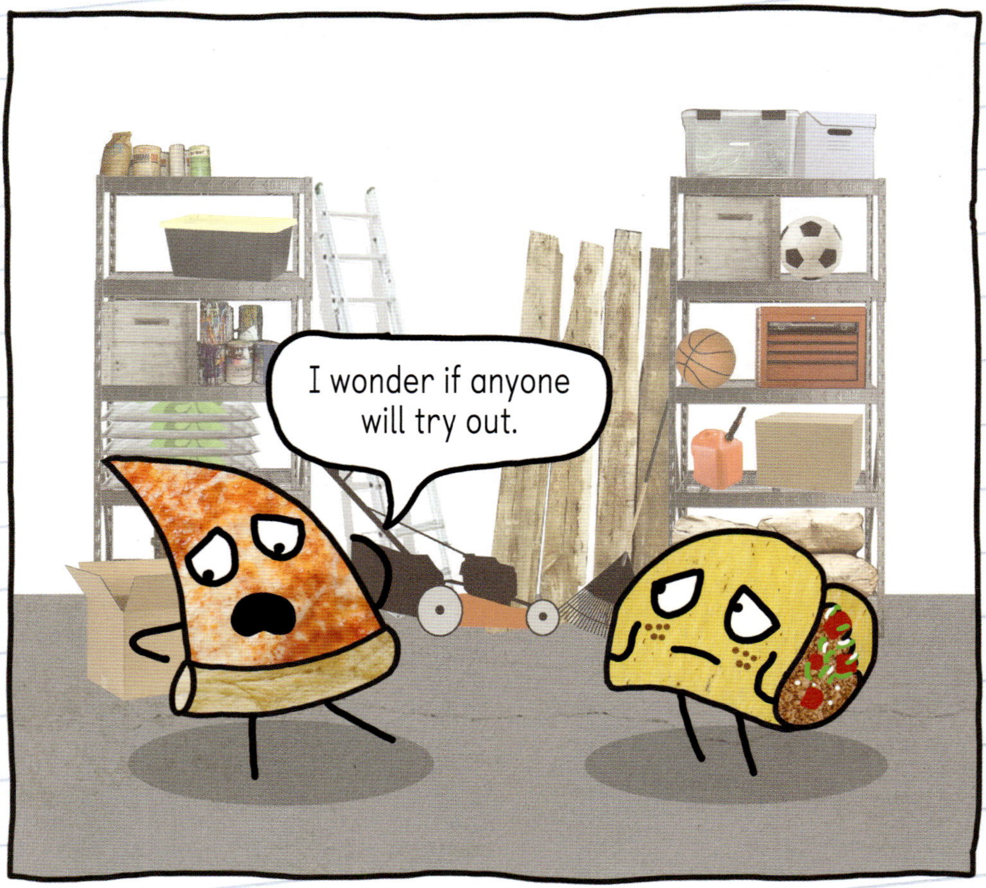
I wonder if anyone will try out.

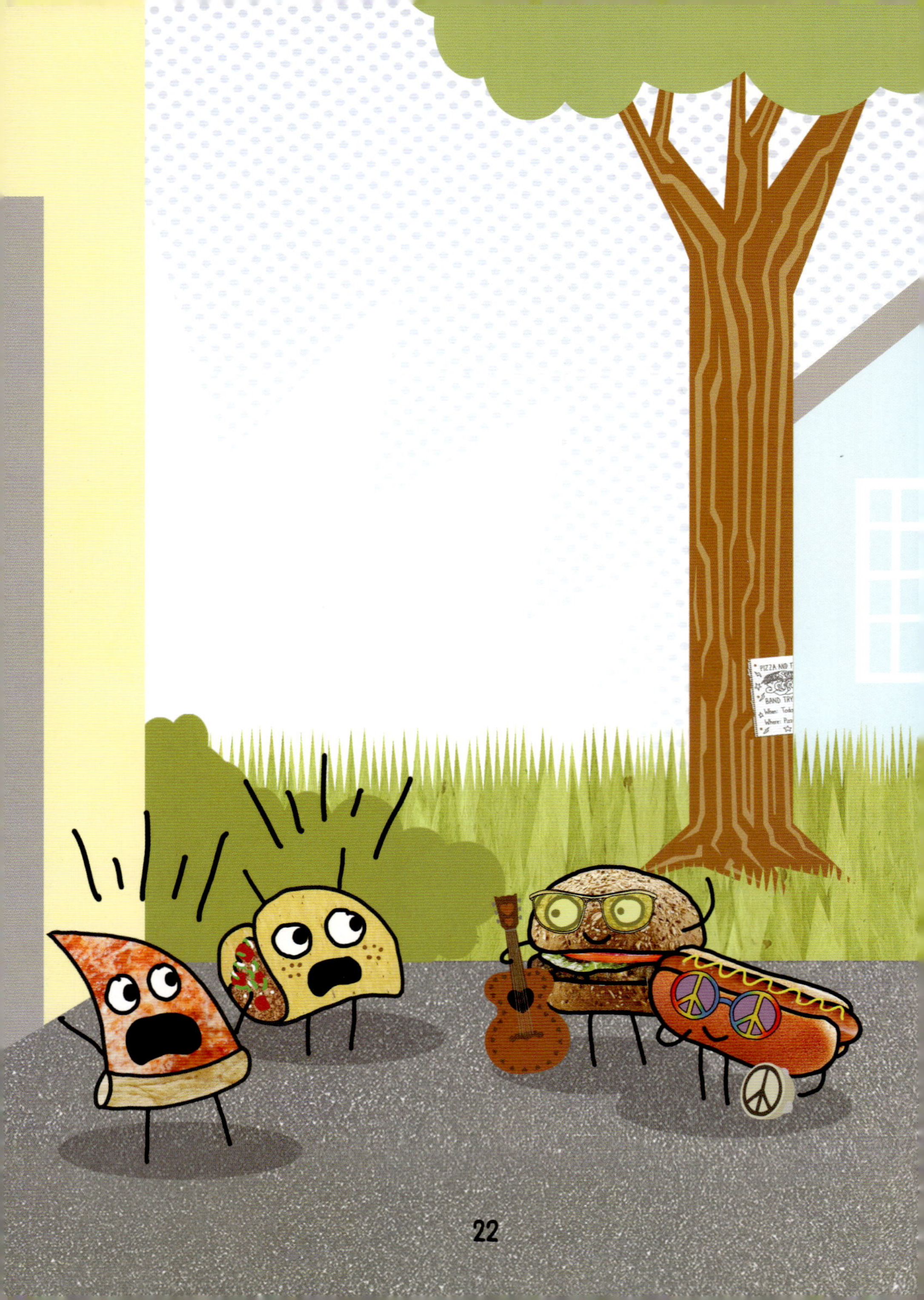

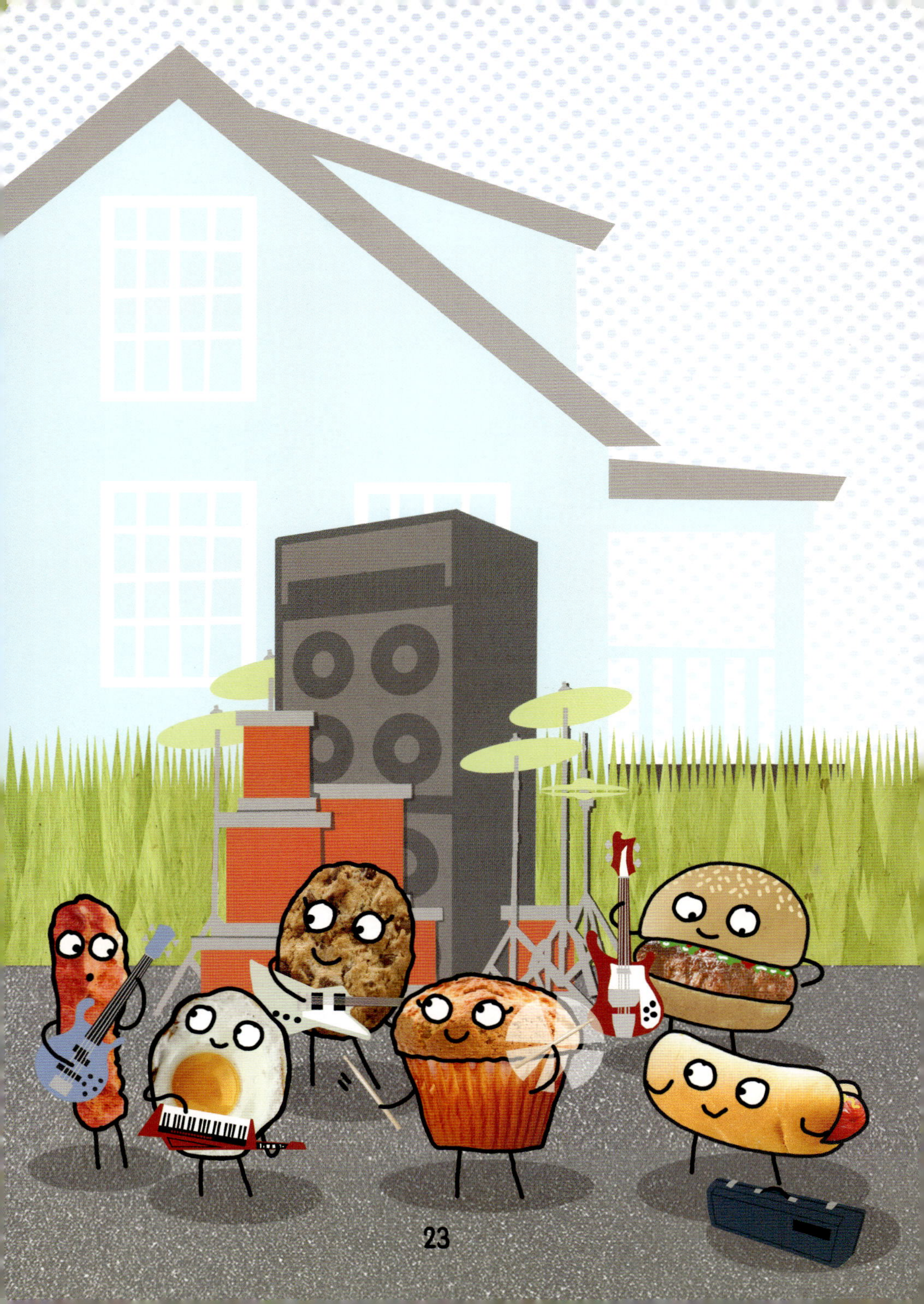

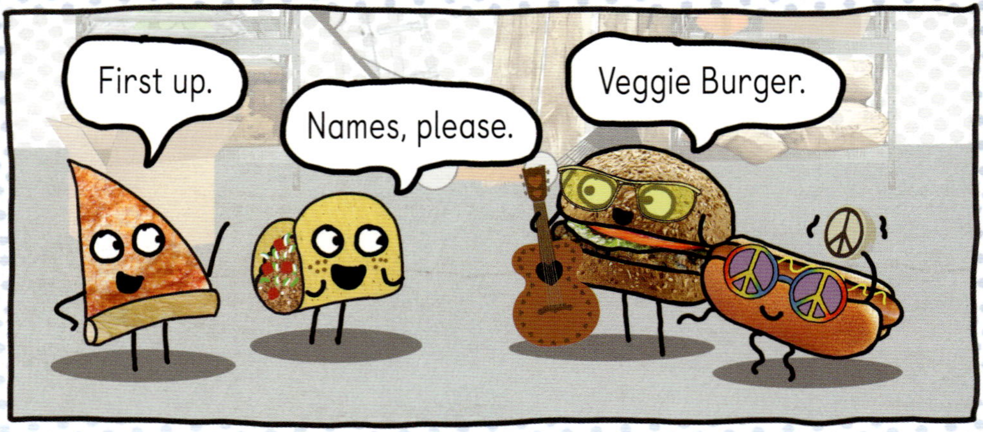
First up.
Names, please.
Veggie Burger.

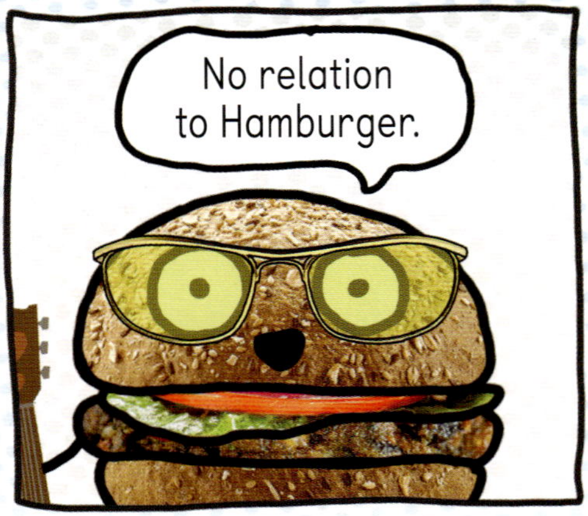
No relation to Hamburger.

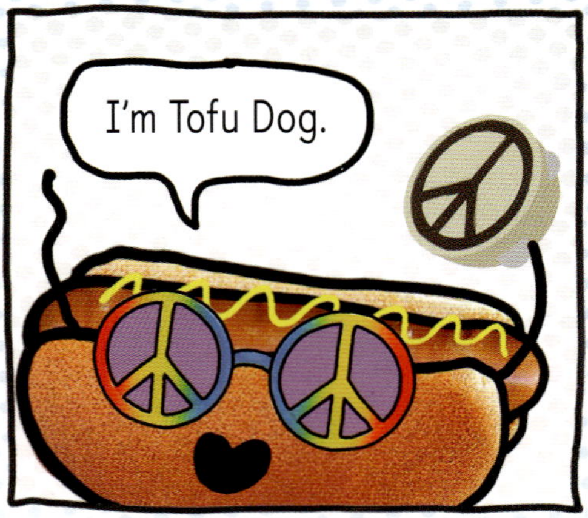
I'm Tofu Dog.

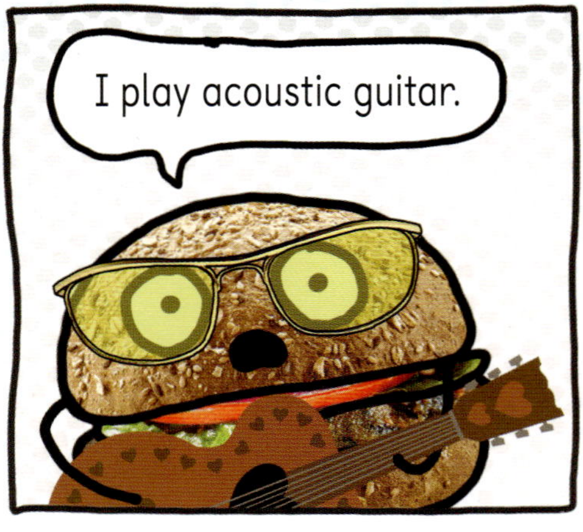
I play acoustic guitar.

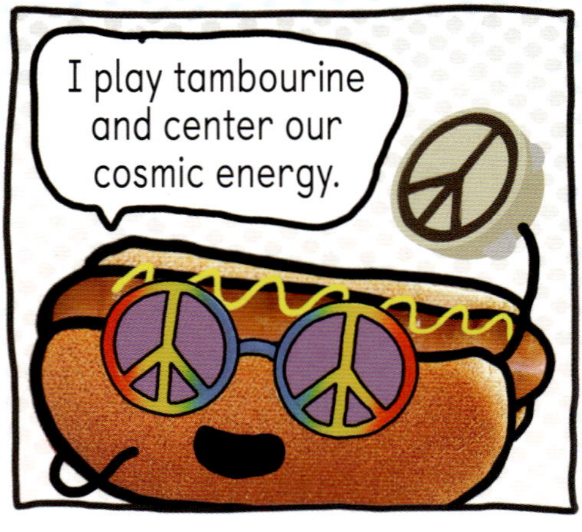
I play tambourine and center our cosmic energy.

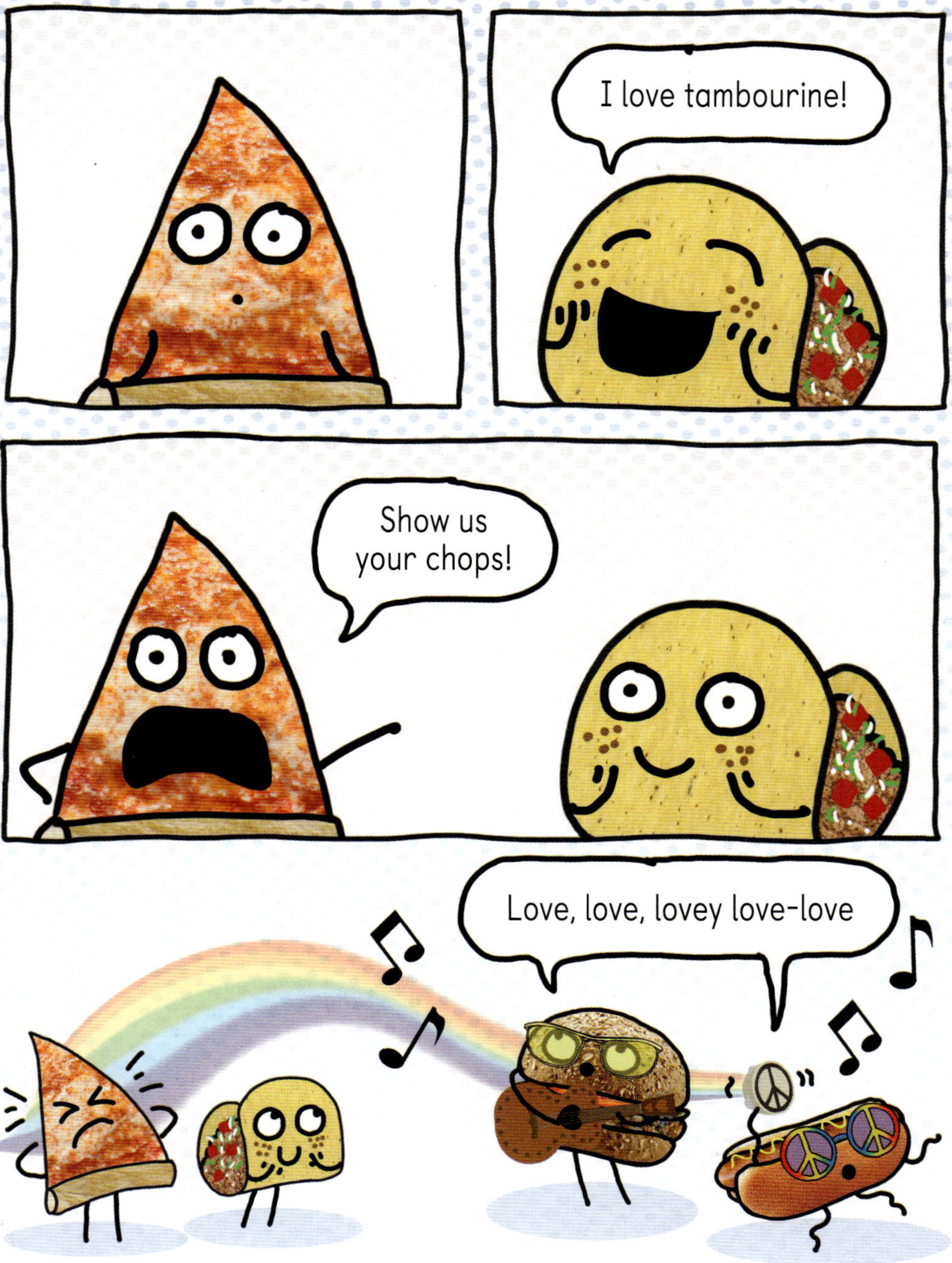
I love tambourine!
Show us your chops!
Love, love, lovey love-love

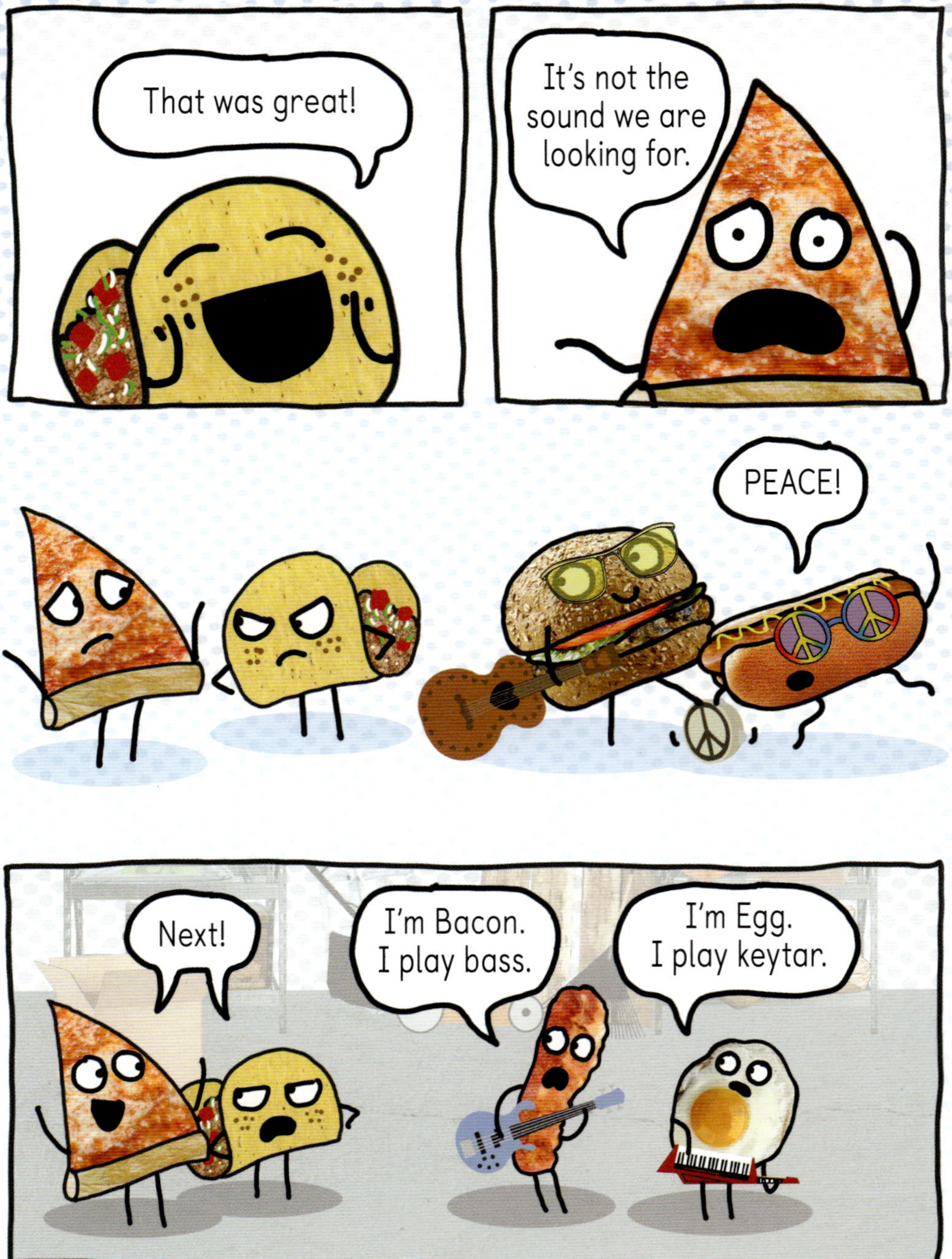
That was great!
It's not the sound we are looking for.
PEACE!
Next!
I'm Bacon. I play bass.
I'm Egg. I play keytar.

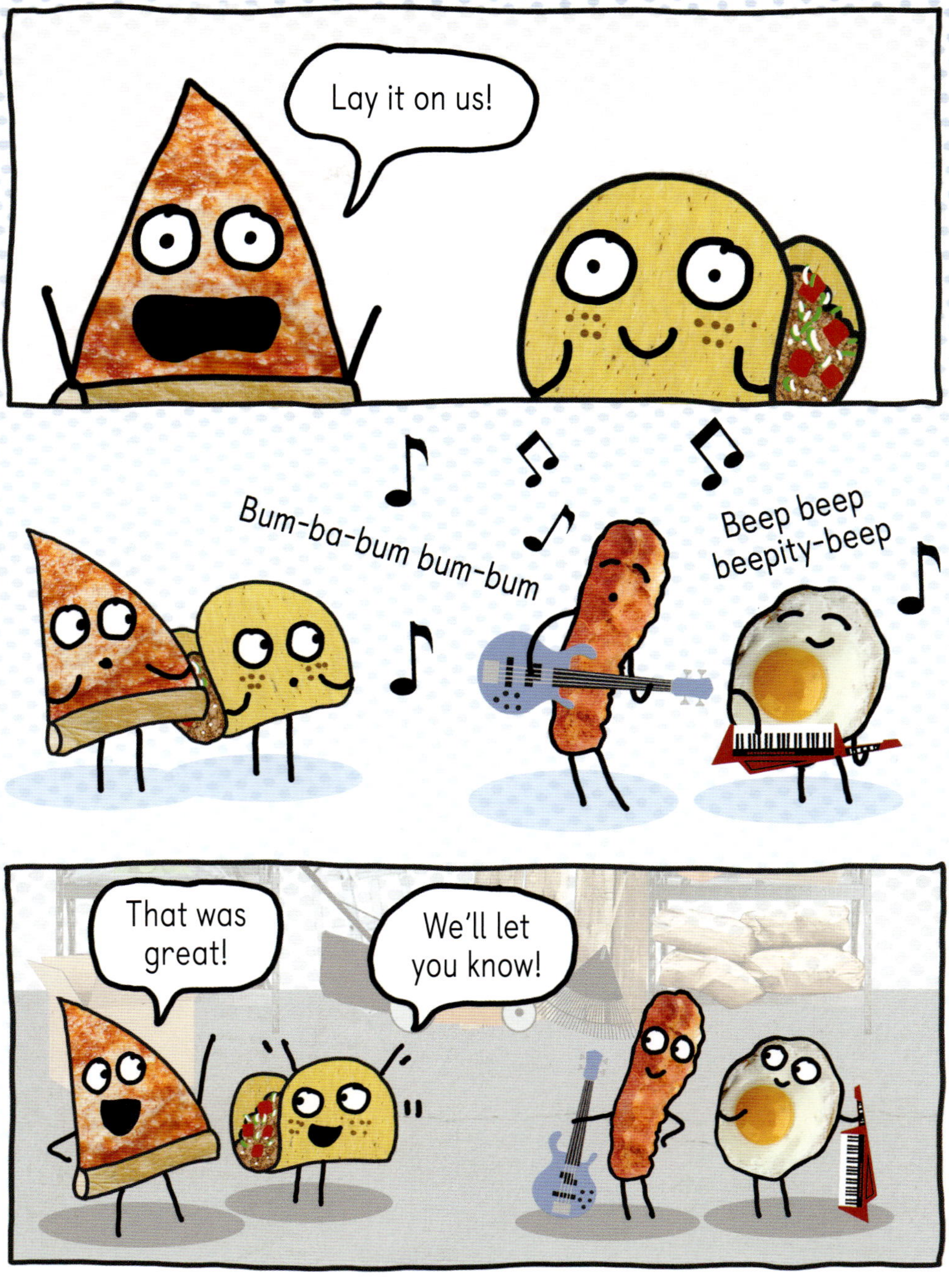

Lay it on us!
Bum-ba-bum bum-bum
Beep beep
beepity-beep
That was
great!
We'll let
you know!

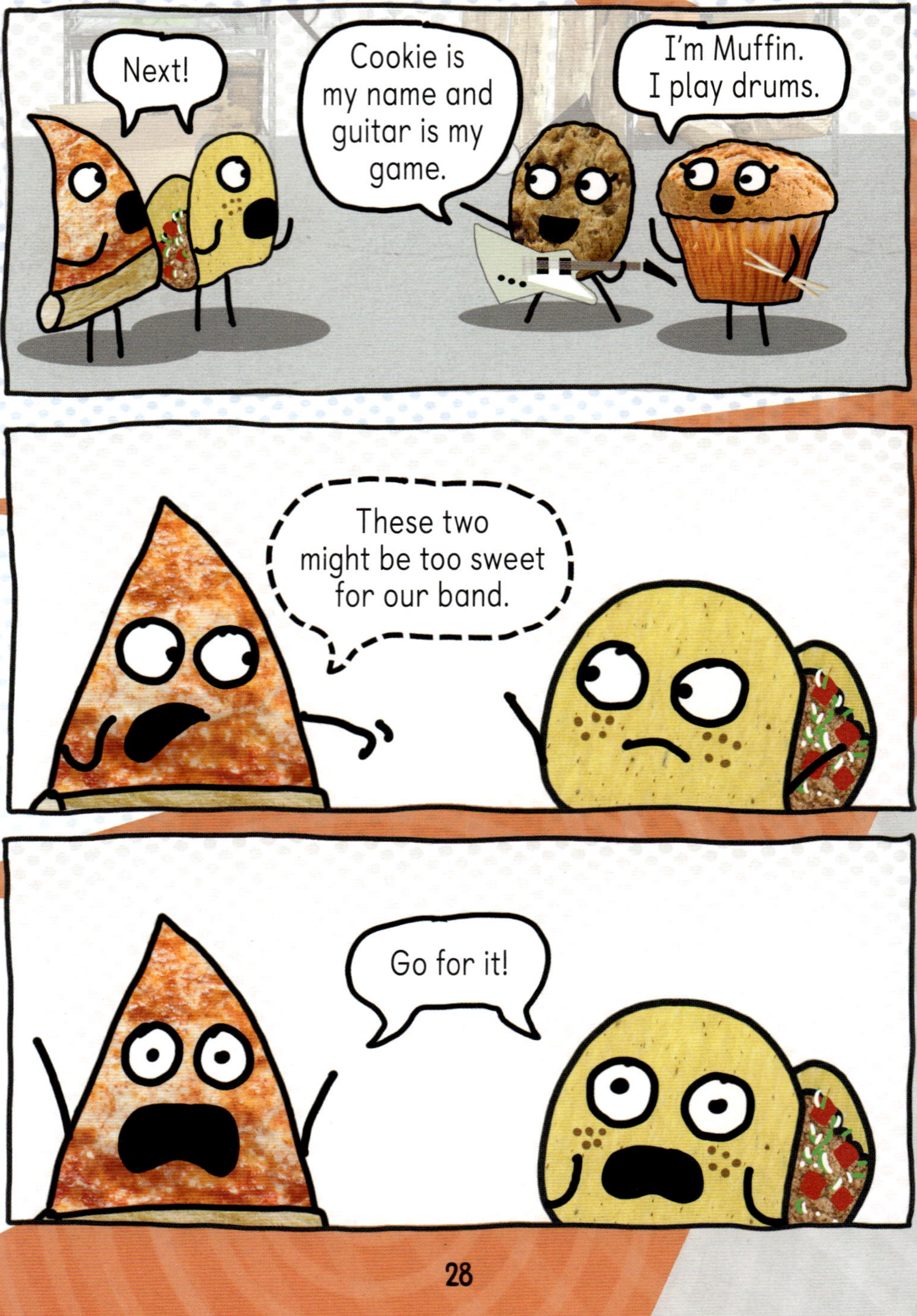
Next!
Cookie is my name and guitar is my game.
I'm Muffin. I play drums.
These two might be too sweet for our band.
Go for it!

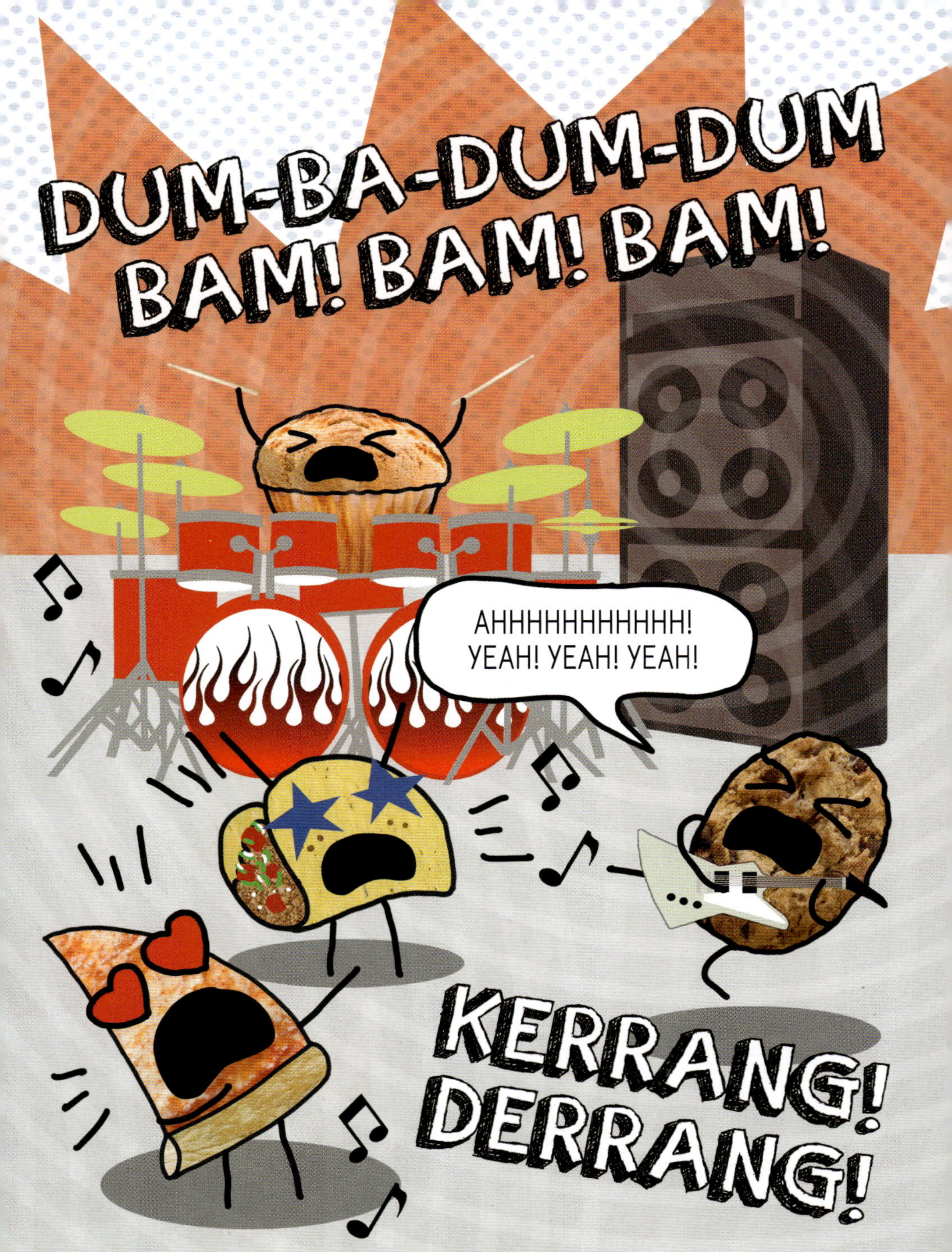
DUM-BA-DUM-DUM
BAM! BAM! BAM!
AHHHHHHHHHHH!
YEAH! YEAH! YEAH!
KERRANG!
DERRANG!

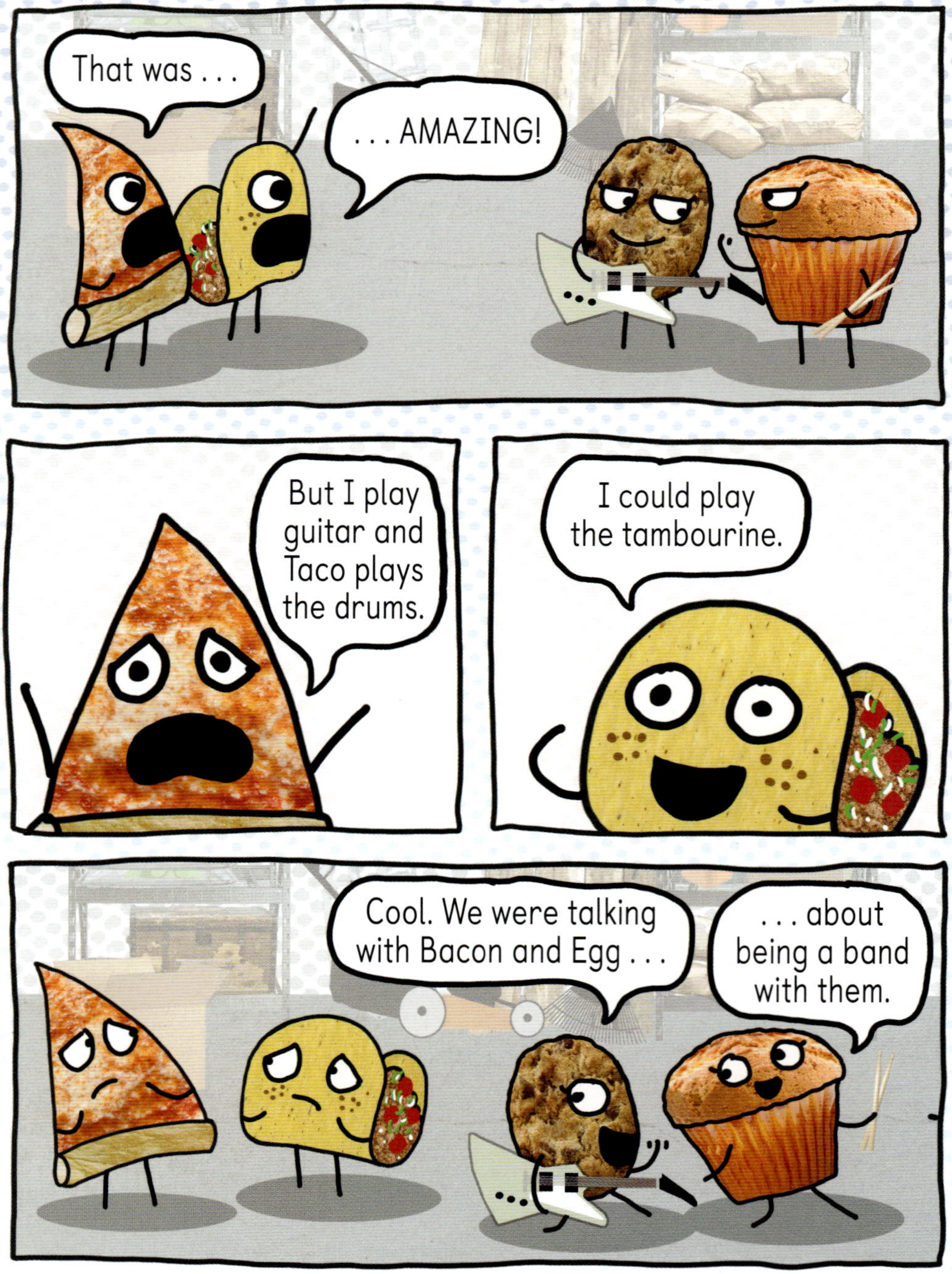
That was . . .
. . . AMAZING!
But I play guitar and Taco plays the drums.
I could play the tambourine.
Cool. We were talking with Bacon and Egg . . .
. . . about being a band with them.

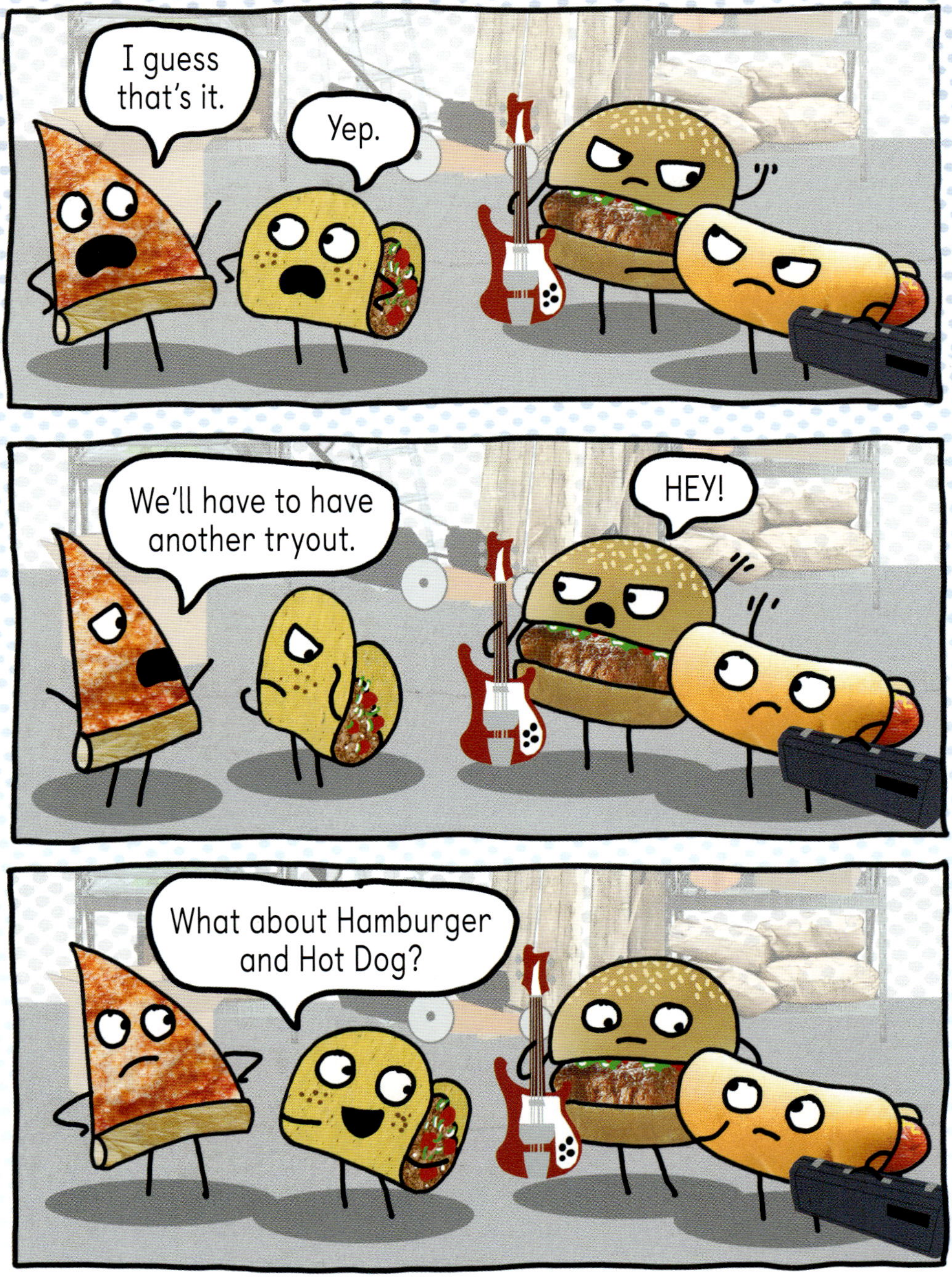
I guess that's it.
Yep.
We'll have to have another tryout.
HEY!
What about Hamburger and Hot Dog?

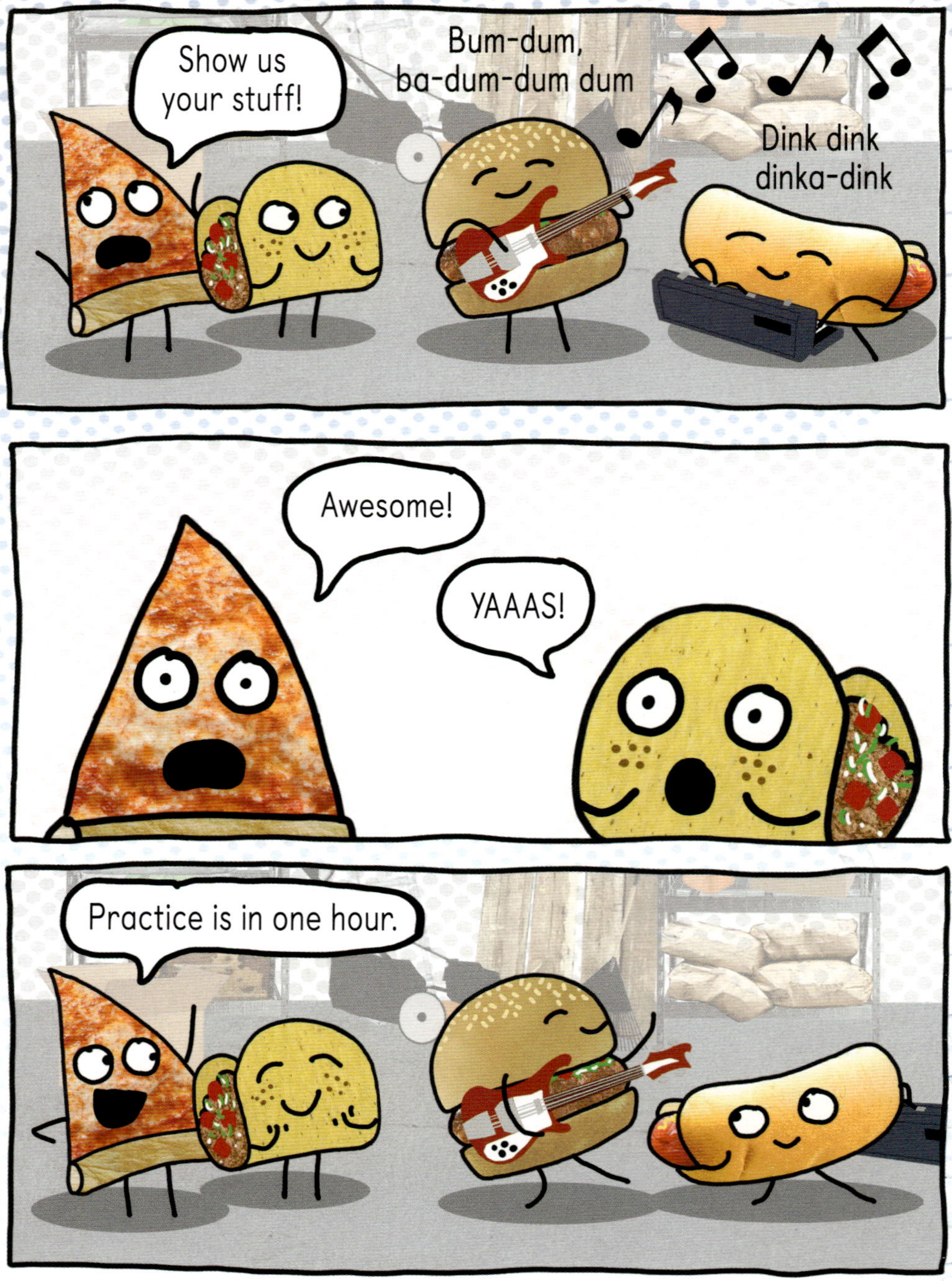
Show us your stuff!
Bum-dum, ba-dum-dum dum
Dink dink dinka-dink
Awesome!
YAAAS!
Practice is in one hour.

Chapter 4

Band Practice

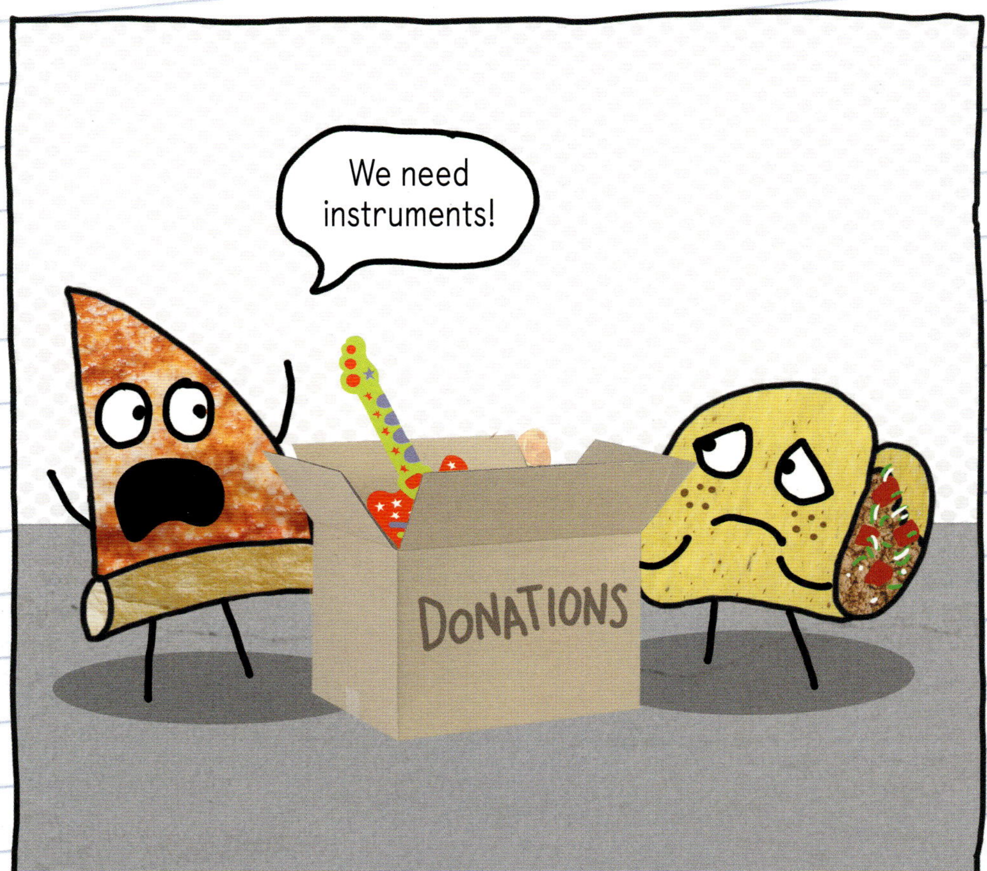

We need instruments!
DONATIONS

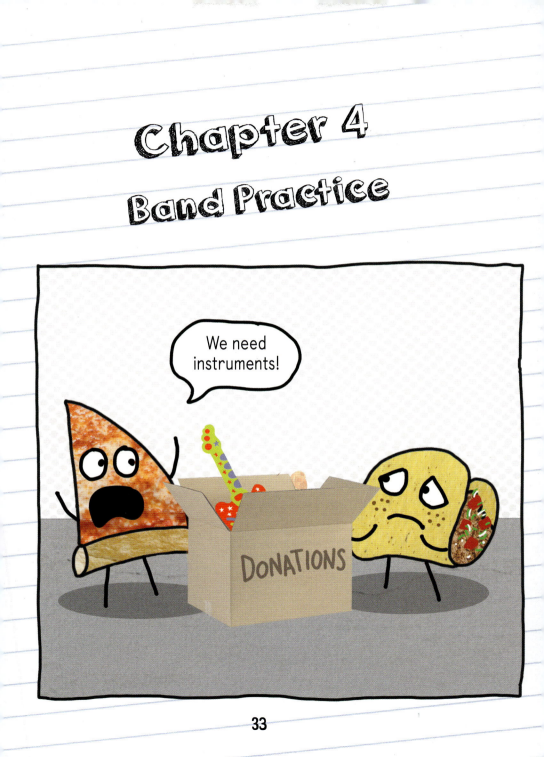

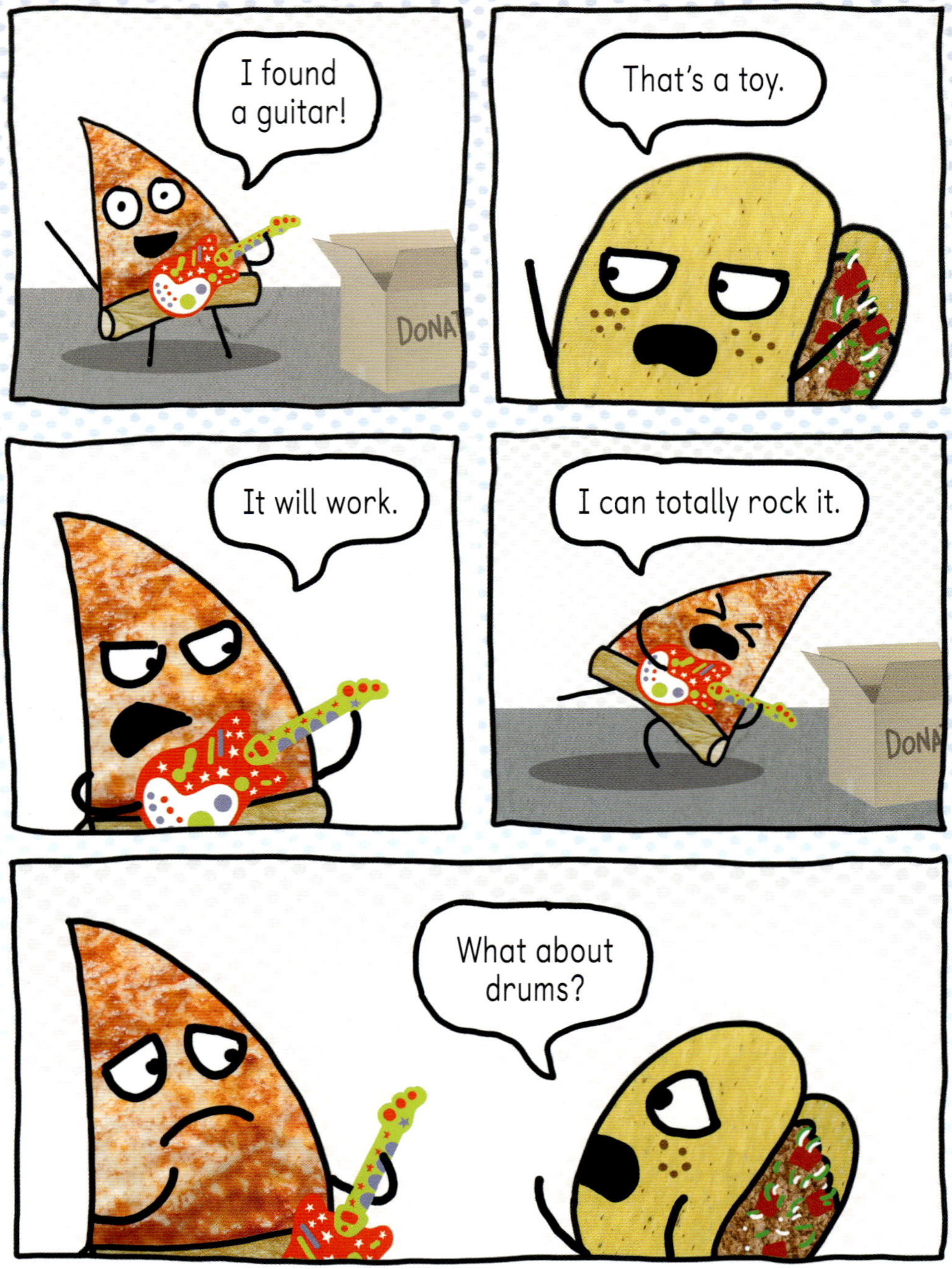
I found a guitar!
That's a toy.
It will work.
I can totally rock it.
DONA
What about drums?

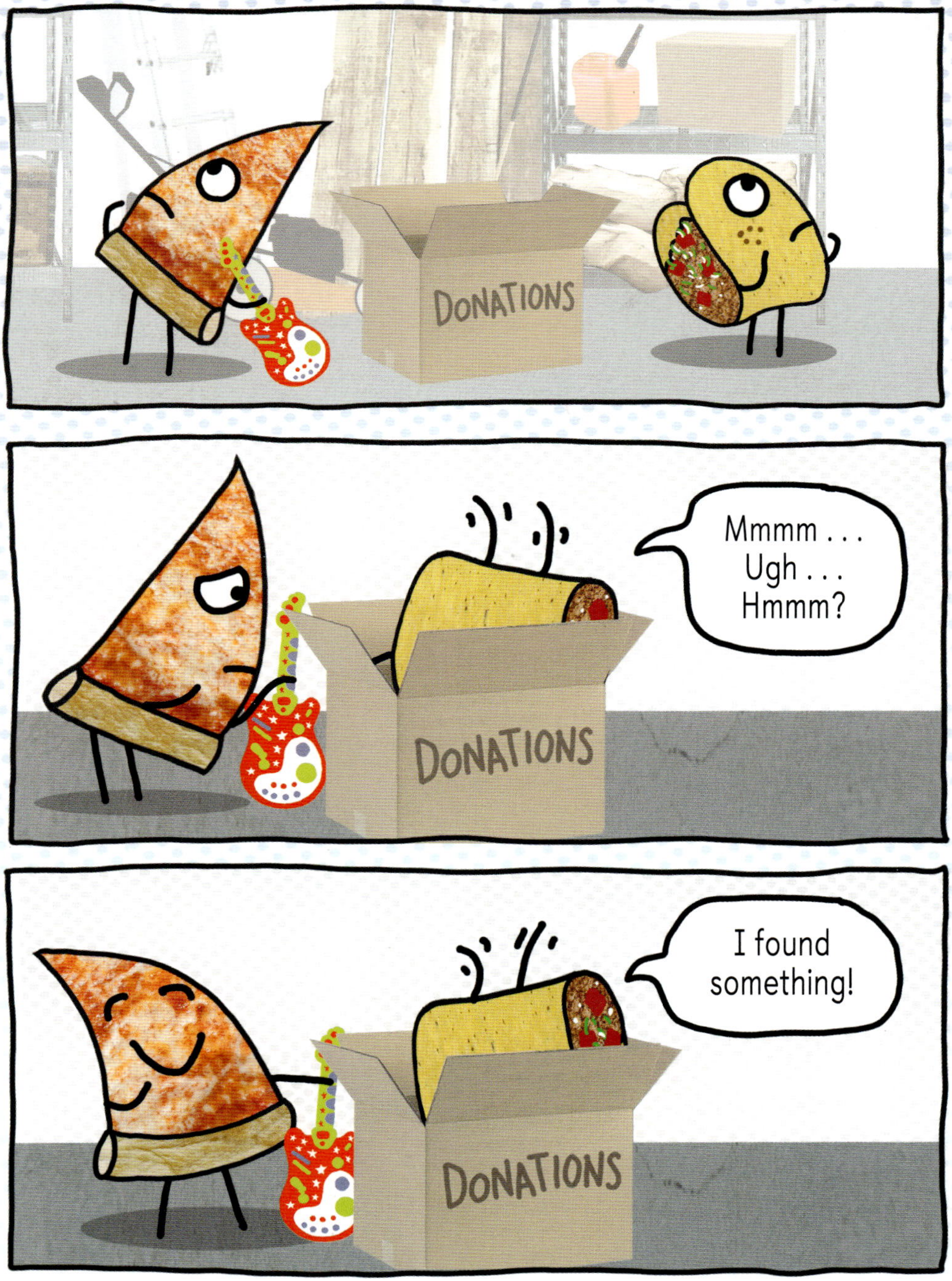
DONATIONS
DONATIONS
Mmmm . . . Ugh . . . Hmmm?
DONATIONS
I found something!

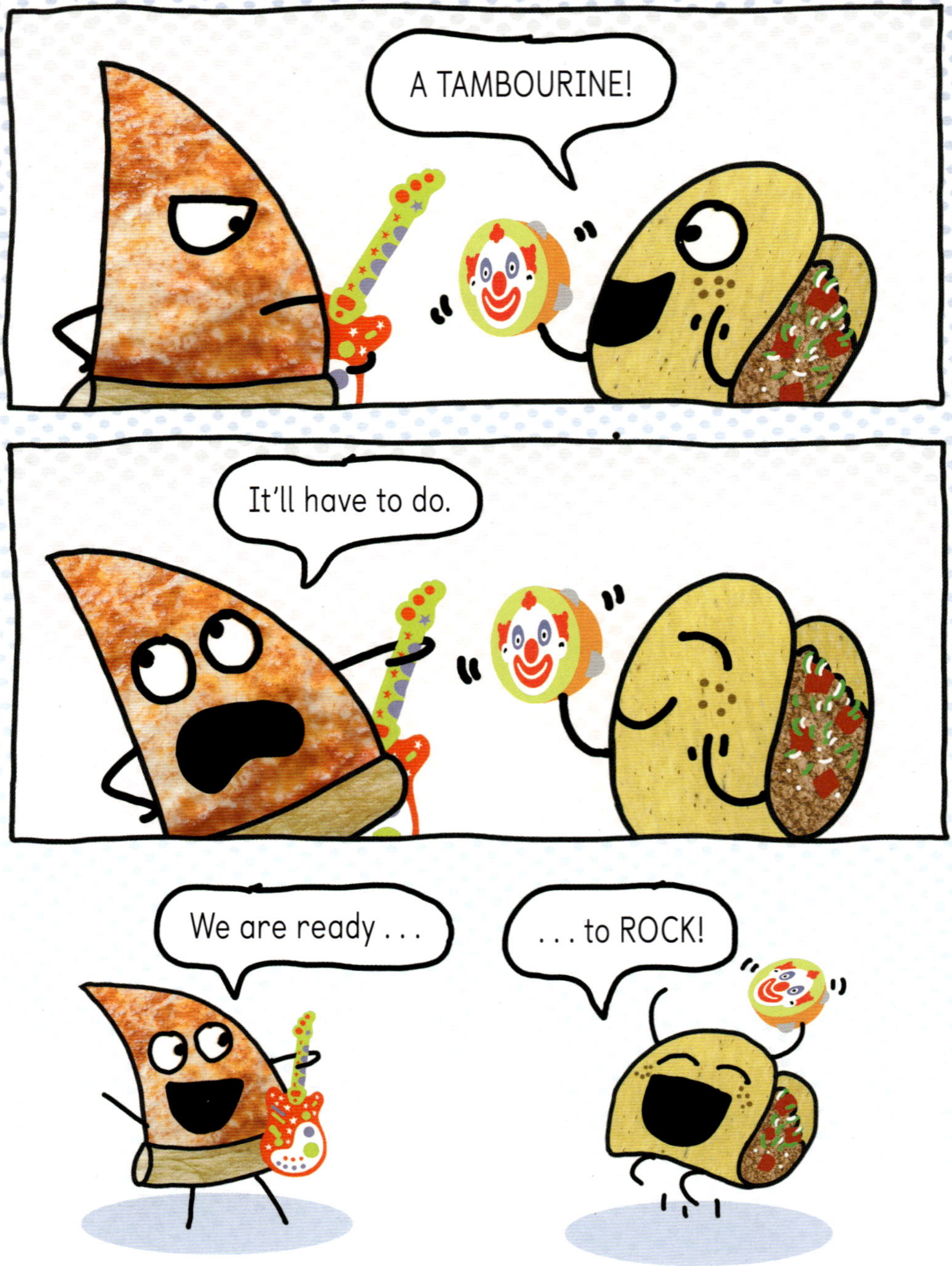
A TAMBOURINE!
It'll have to do.
We are ready . . .
. . . to ROCK!

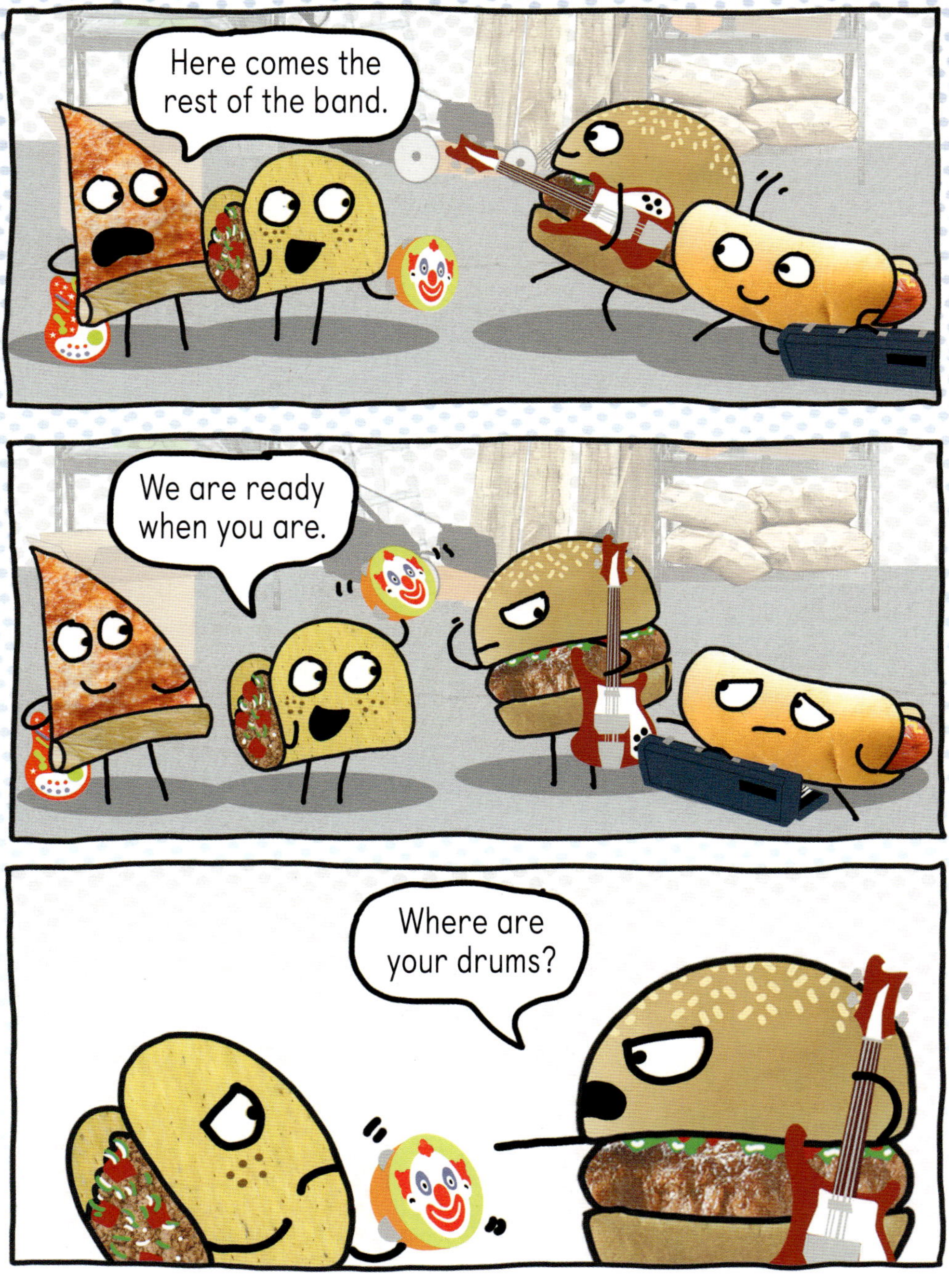
Here comes the rest of the band.
We are ready when you are.
Where are your drums?

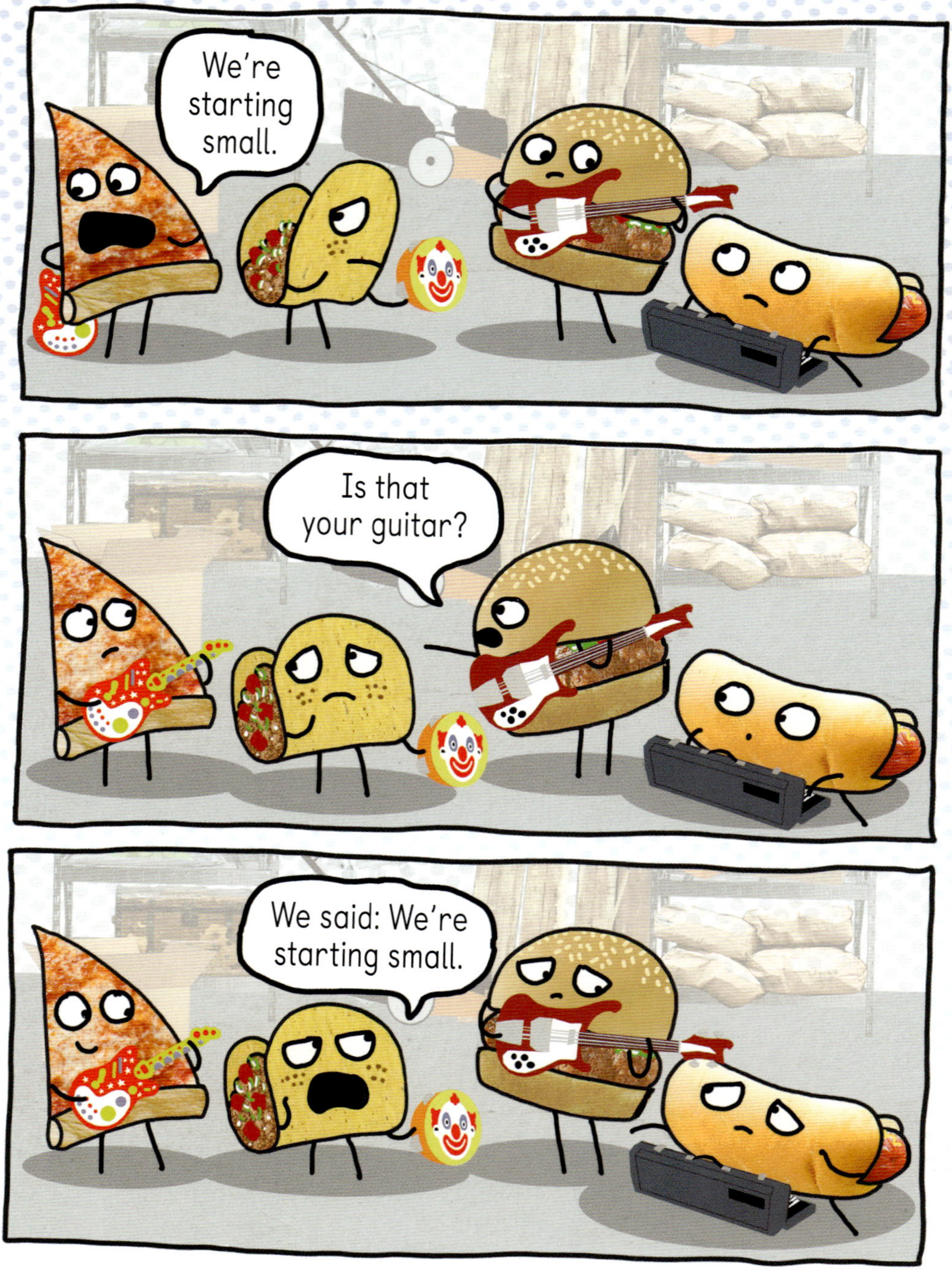
We're starting small.
Is that your guitar?
We said: We're starting small.

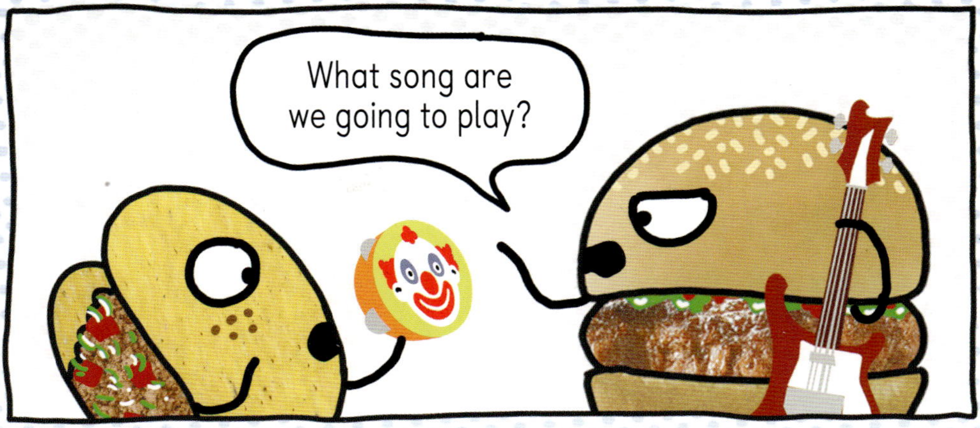
What song are
we going to play?

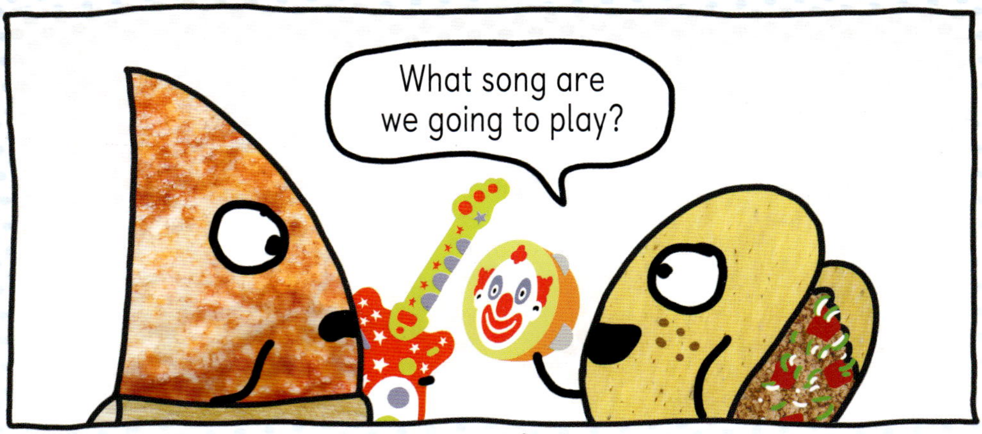
What song are
we going to play?

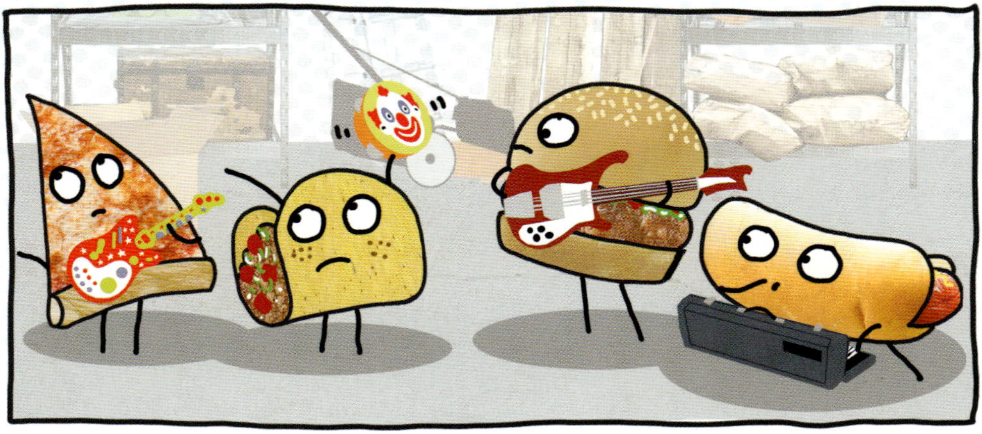

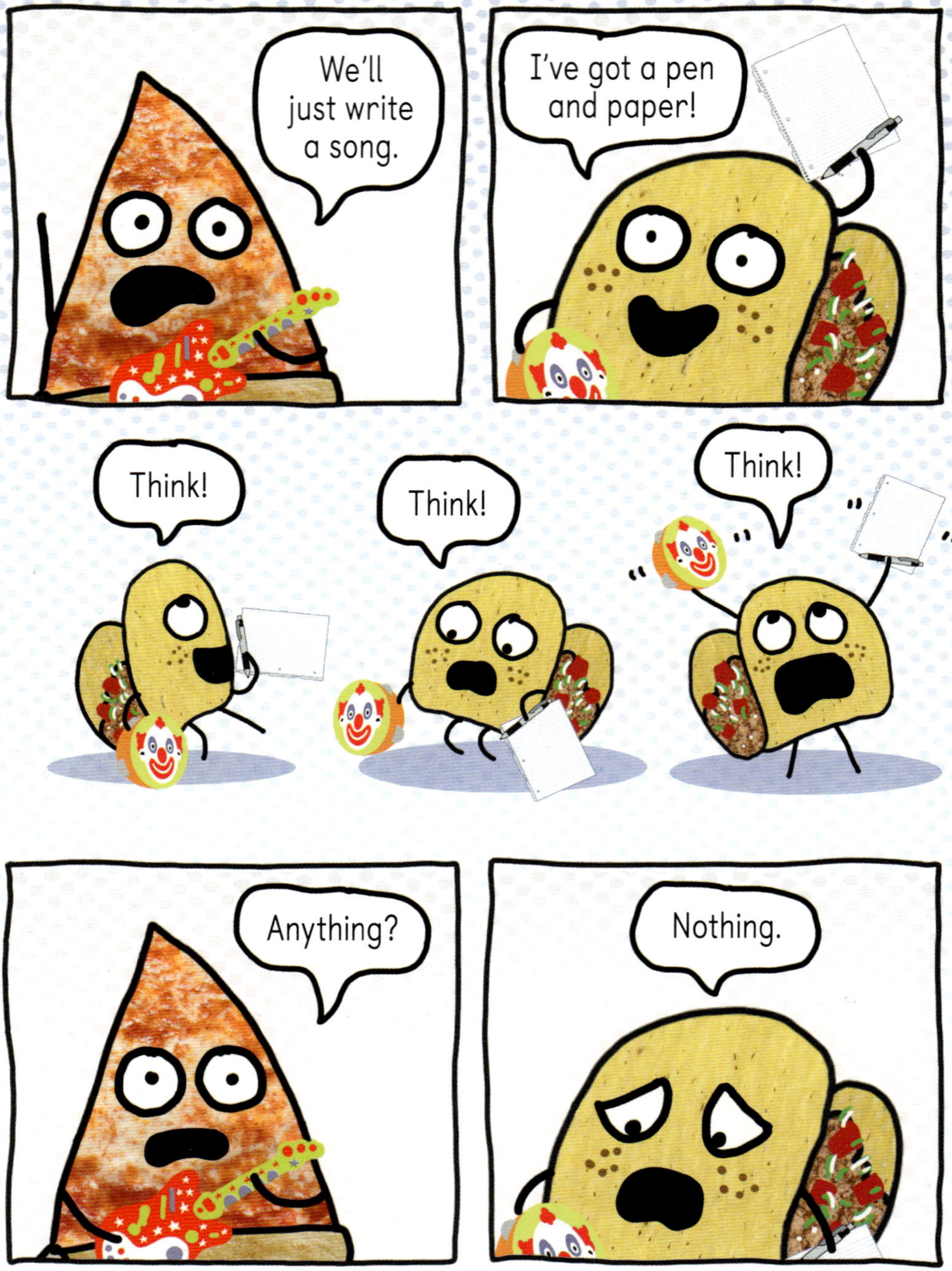
We'll just write a song.
I've got a pen and paper!
Think!
Think!
Think!
Anything?
Nothing.

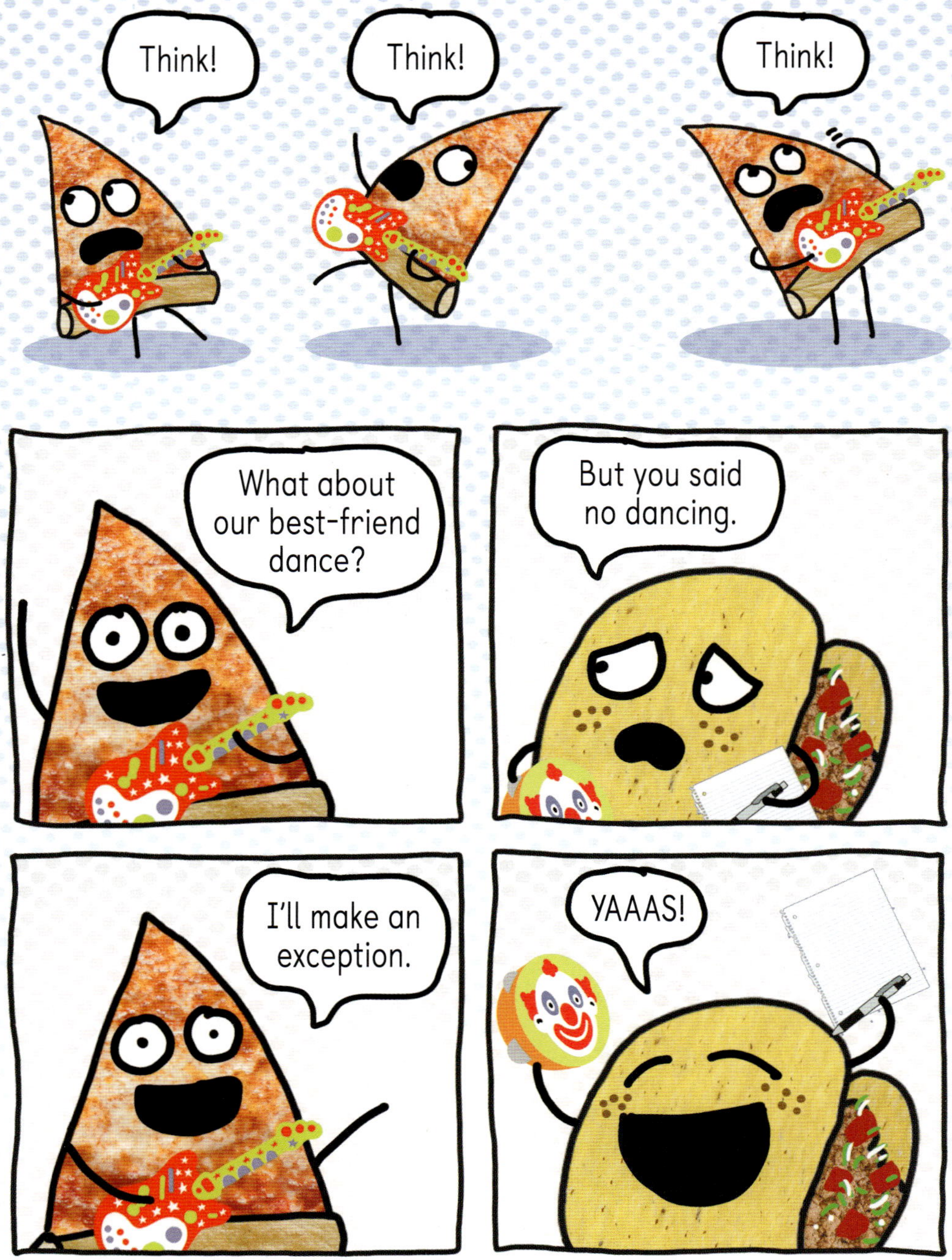
Think!
Think!
Think!
What about our best-friend dance?
But you said no dancing.
I'll make an exception.
YAAAS!

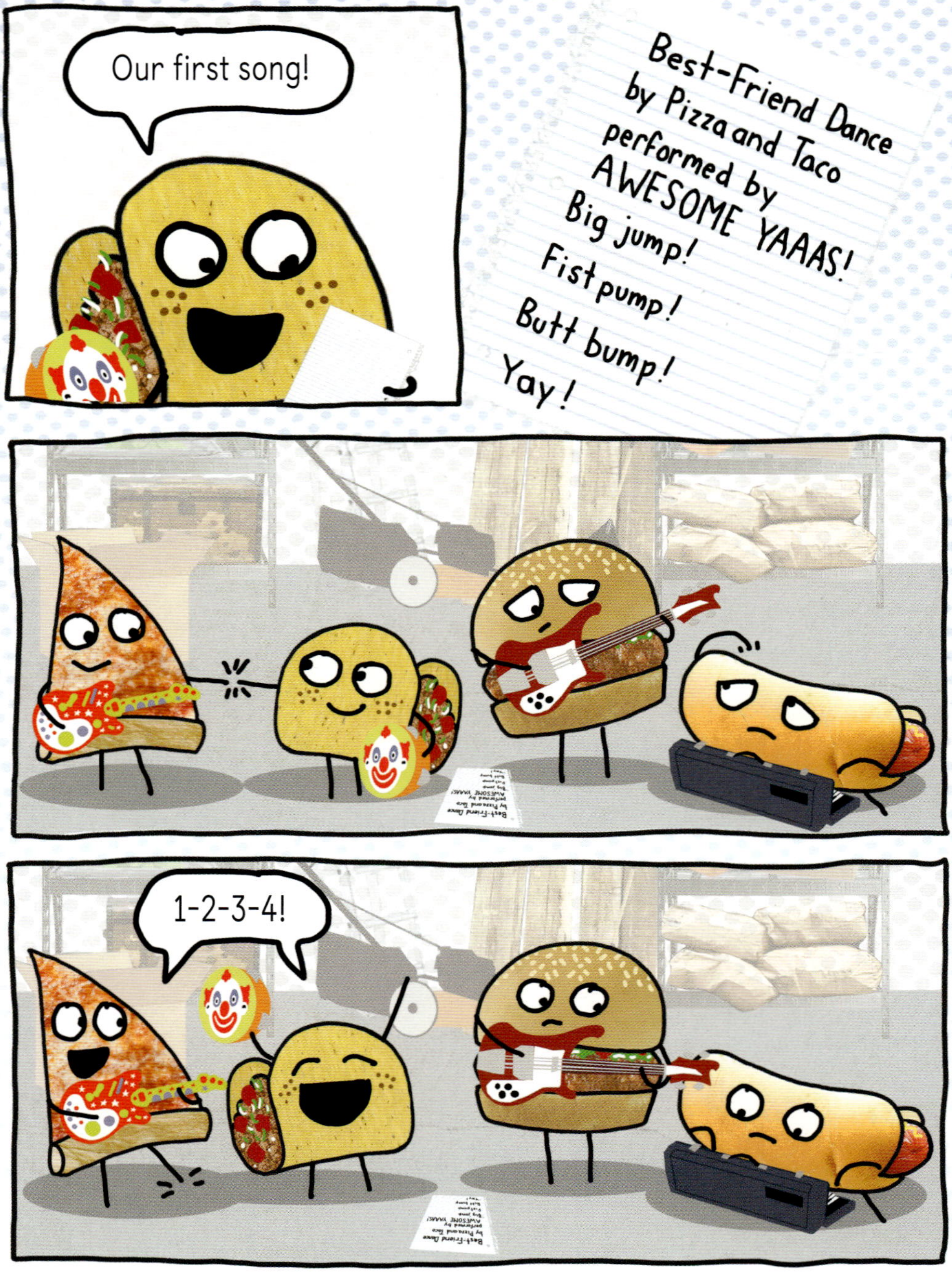
Our first song!
Best-Friend Dance
by Pizza and Taco
performed by
AWESOME YAAAS!
Big jump!
Fist pump!
Butt bump!
Yay!
1-2-3-4!

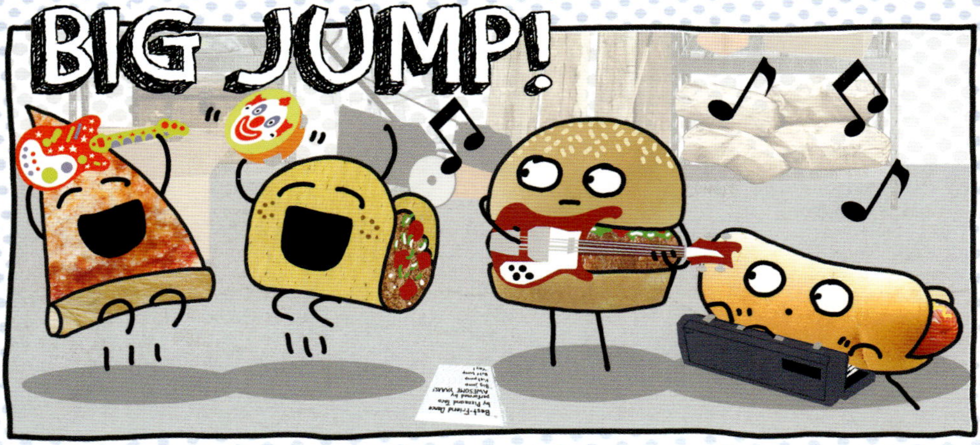
BIG JUMP!

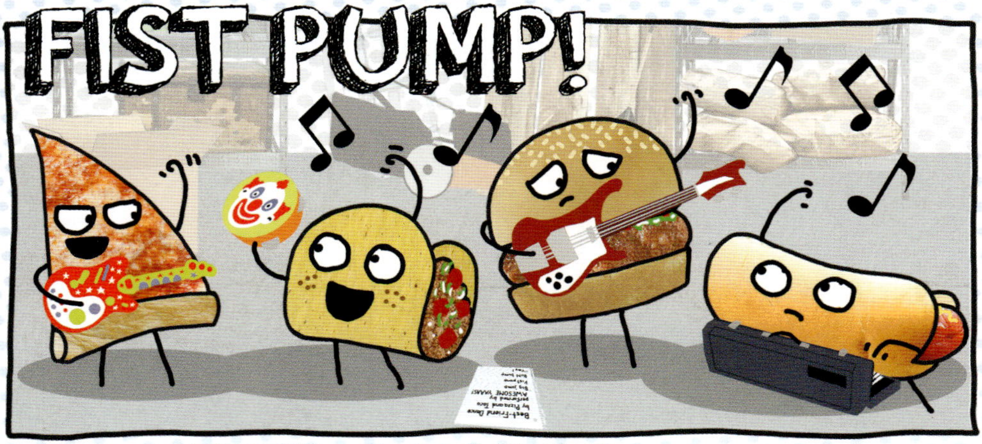
FIST PUMP!

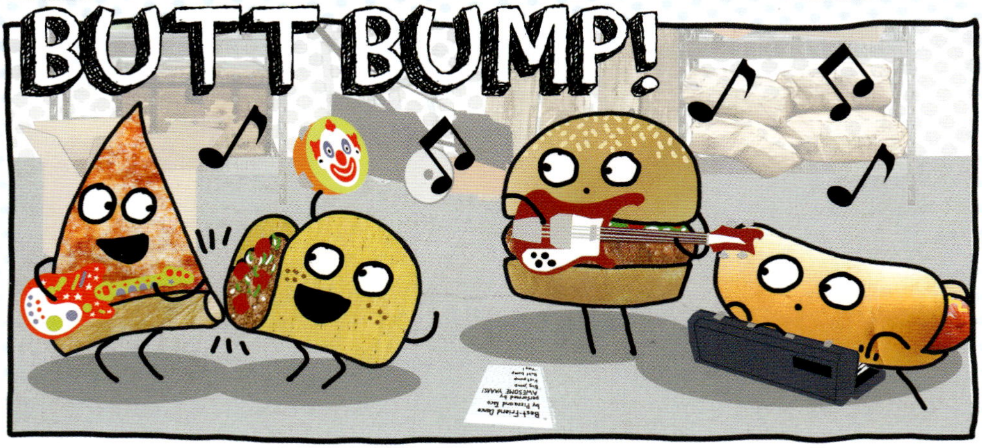
BUTT BUMP!

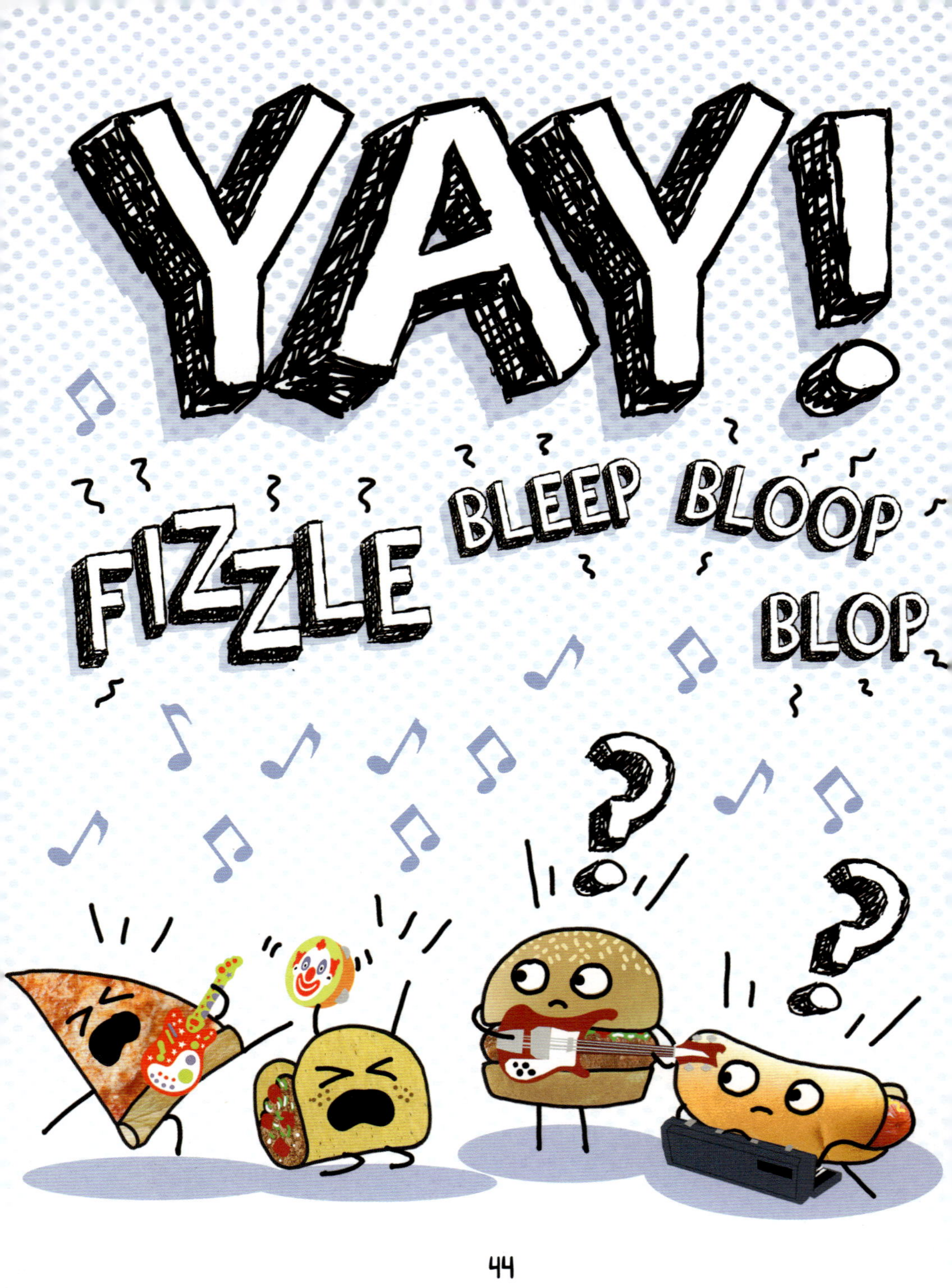
YAY!
FIZZLE
BLEEP
BLOOP
BLOP

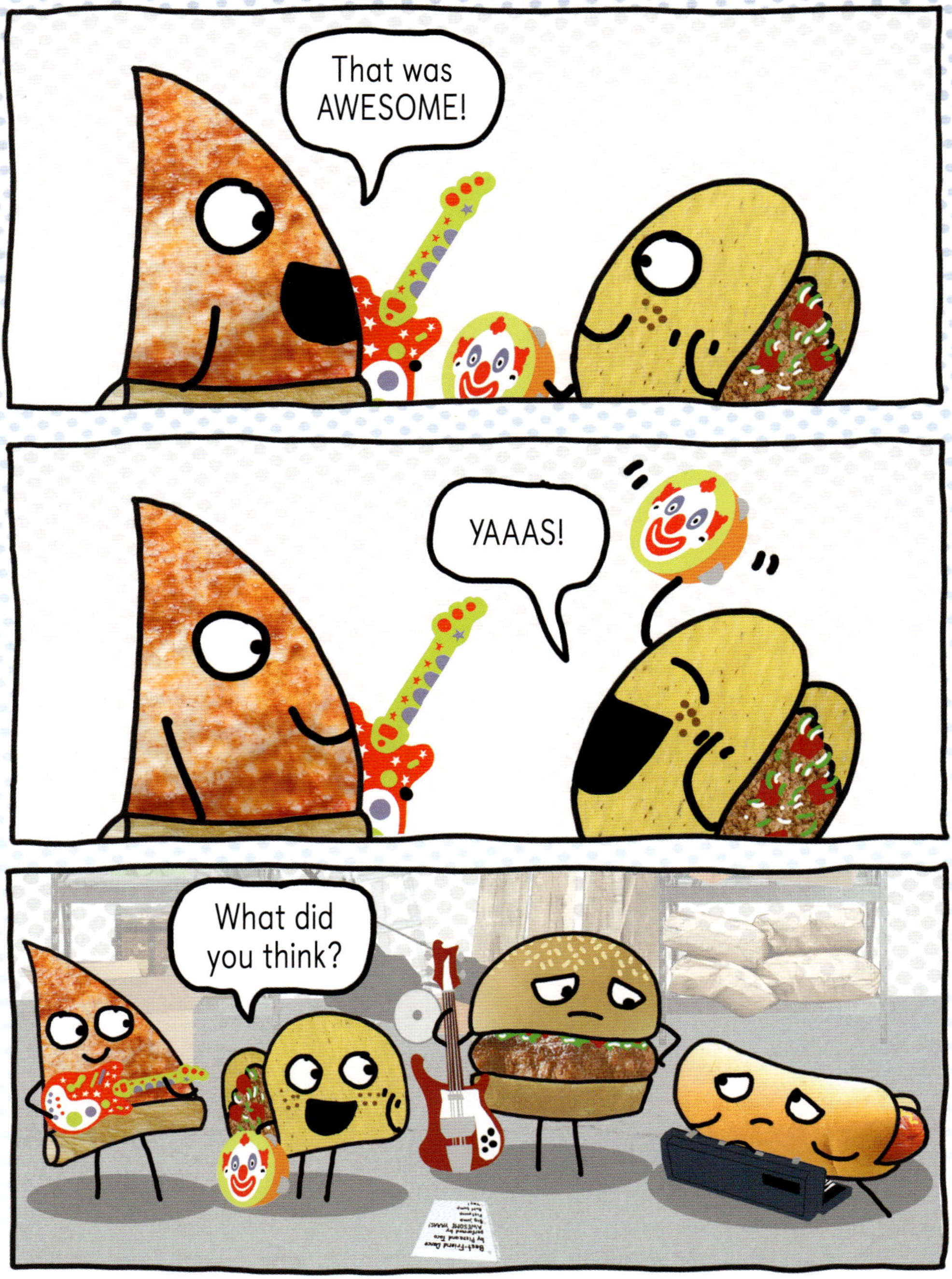
That was AWESOME!
YAAAS!
What did you think?

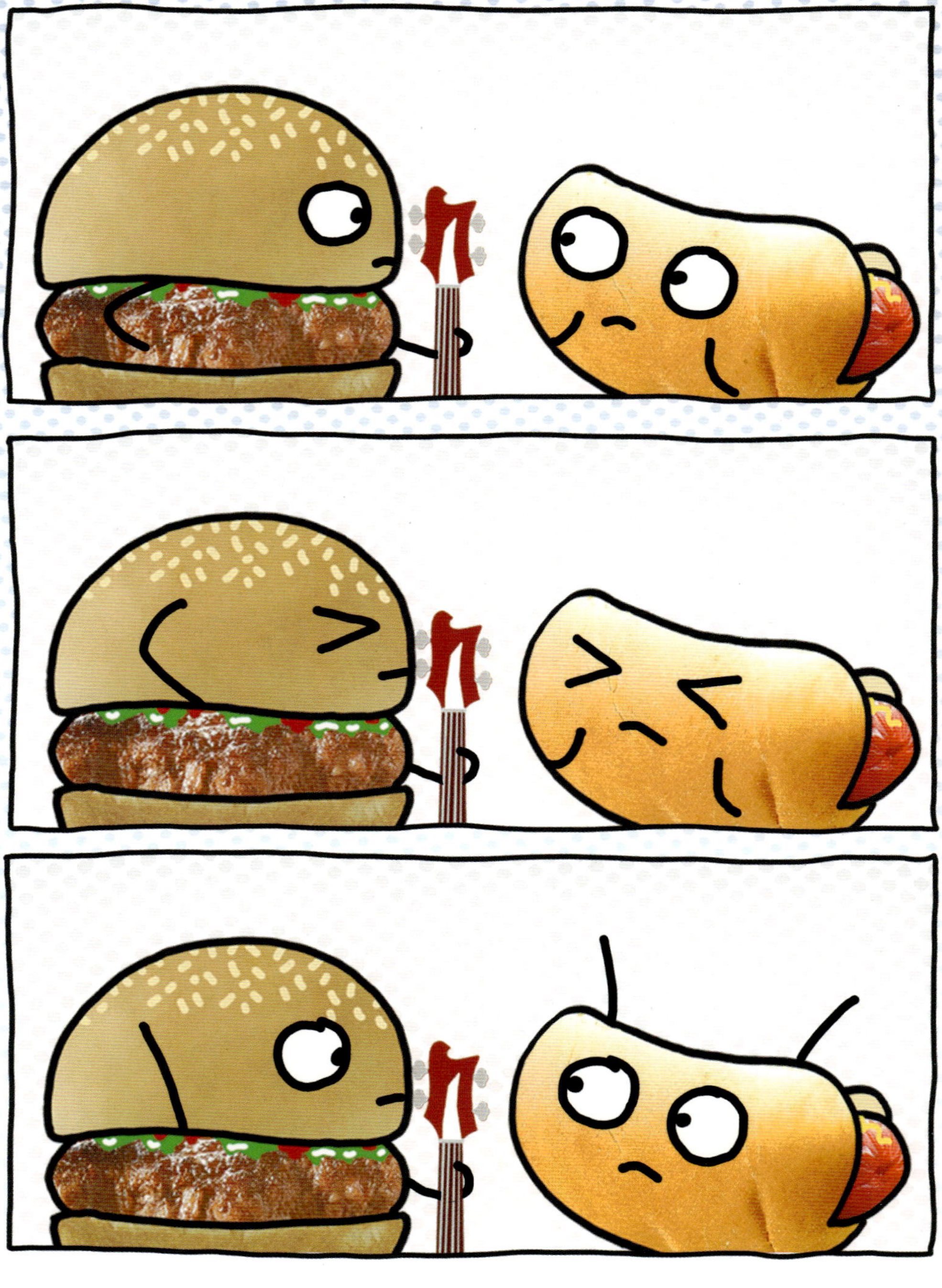

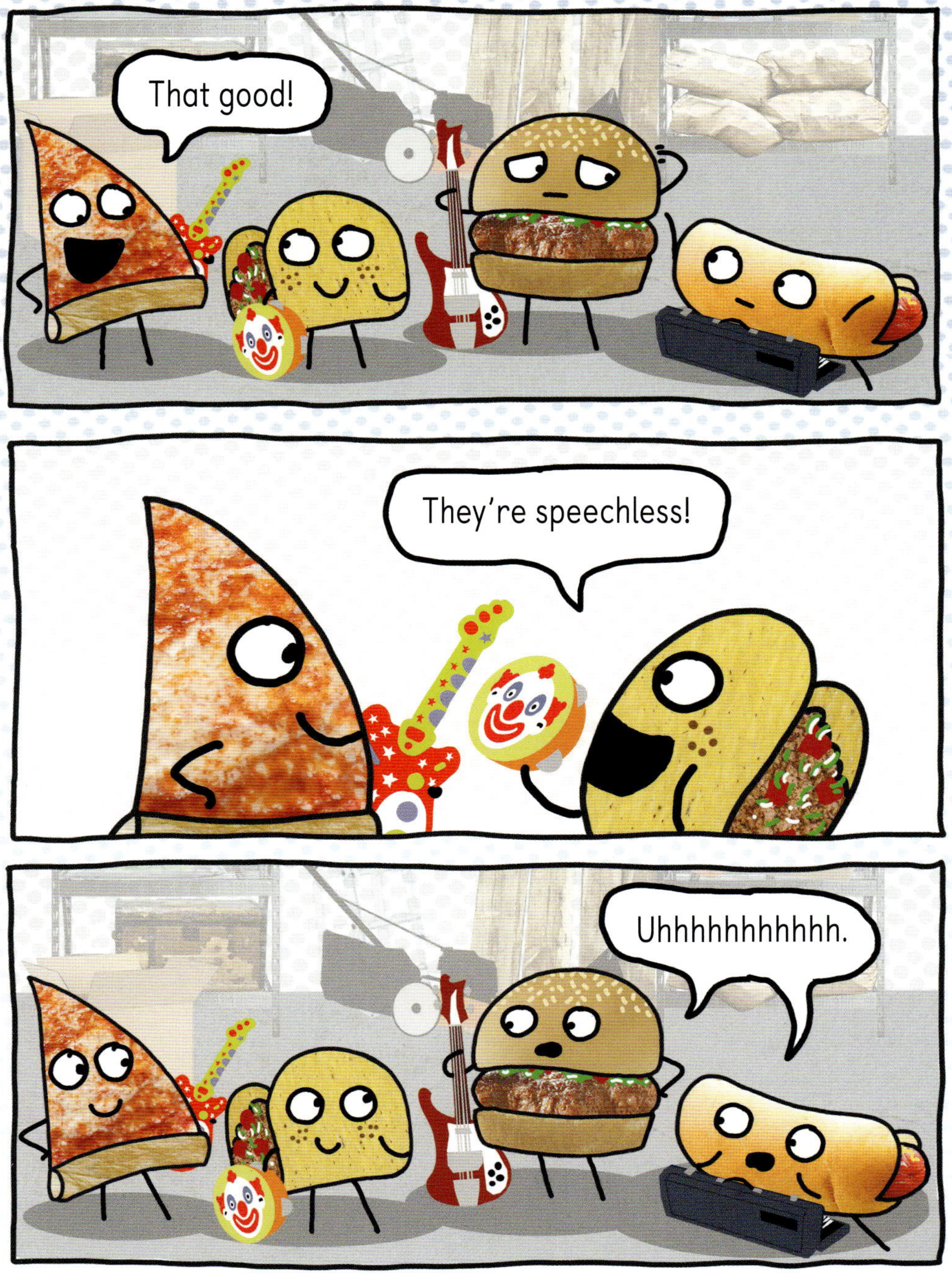
That good!
They're speechless!
Uhhhhhhhhhhh.

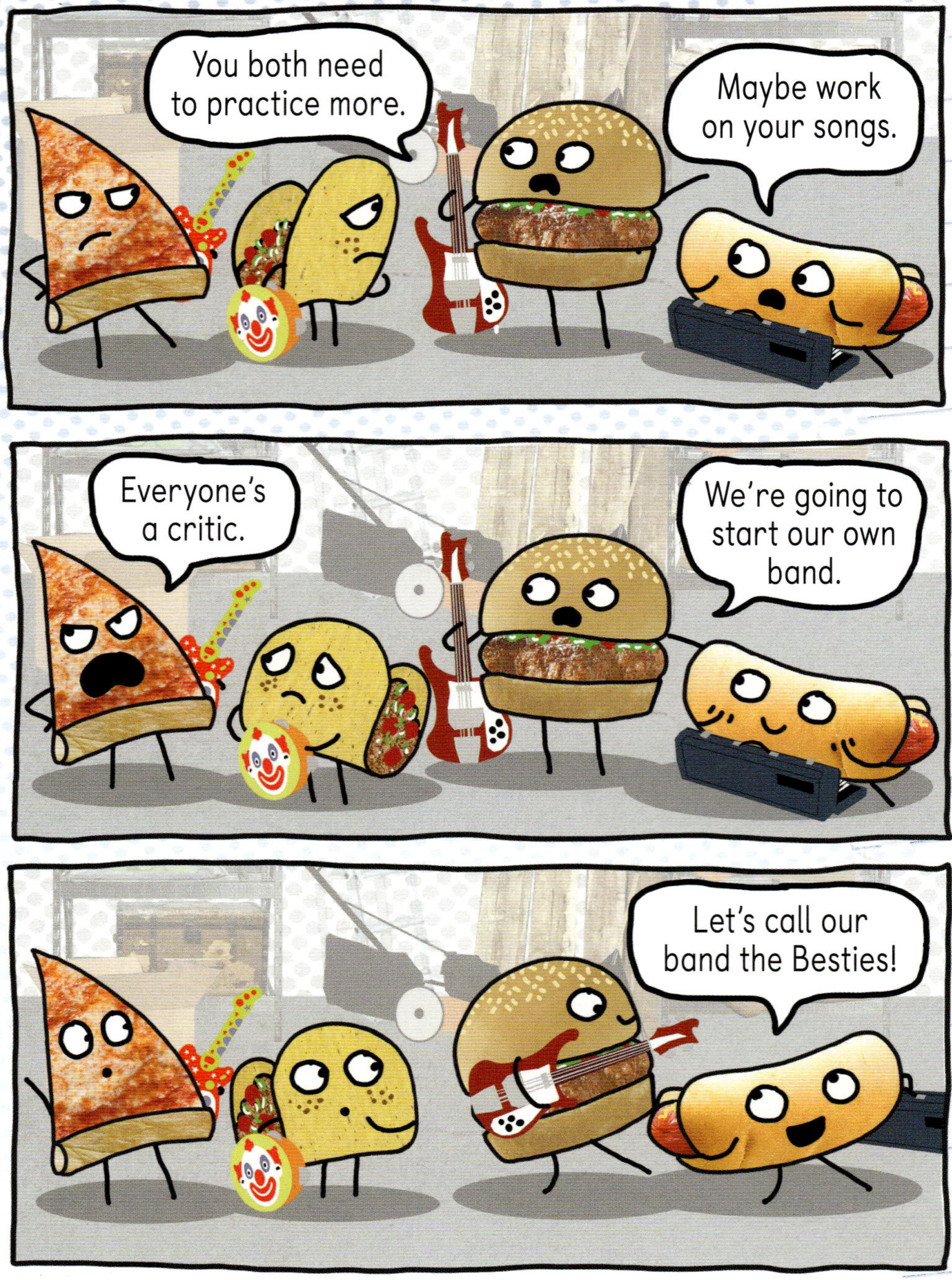
You both need to practice more.
Maybe work on your songs.
Everyone's a critic.
We're going to start our own band.
Let's call our band the Besties!

Chapter 5

What Now?

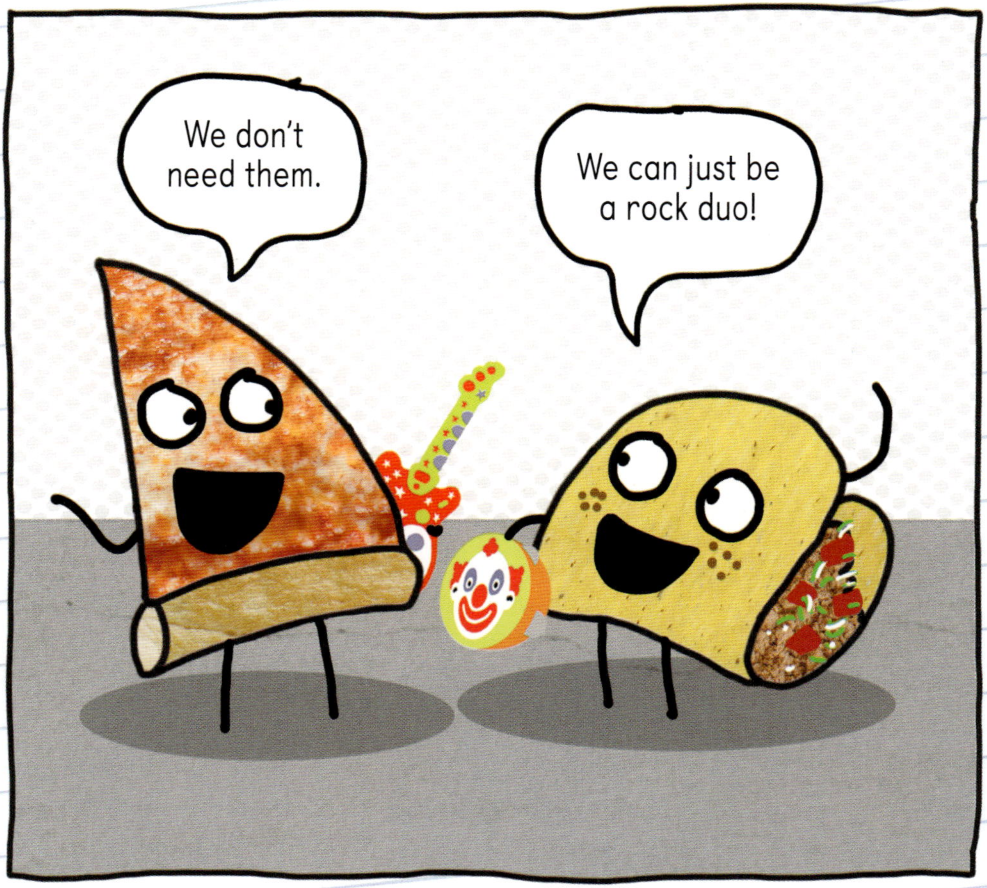
We don't need them.
We can just be a rock duo!

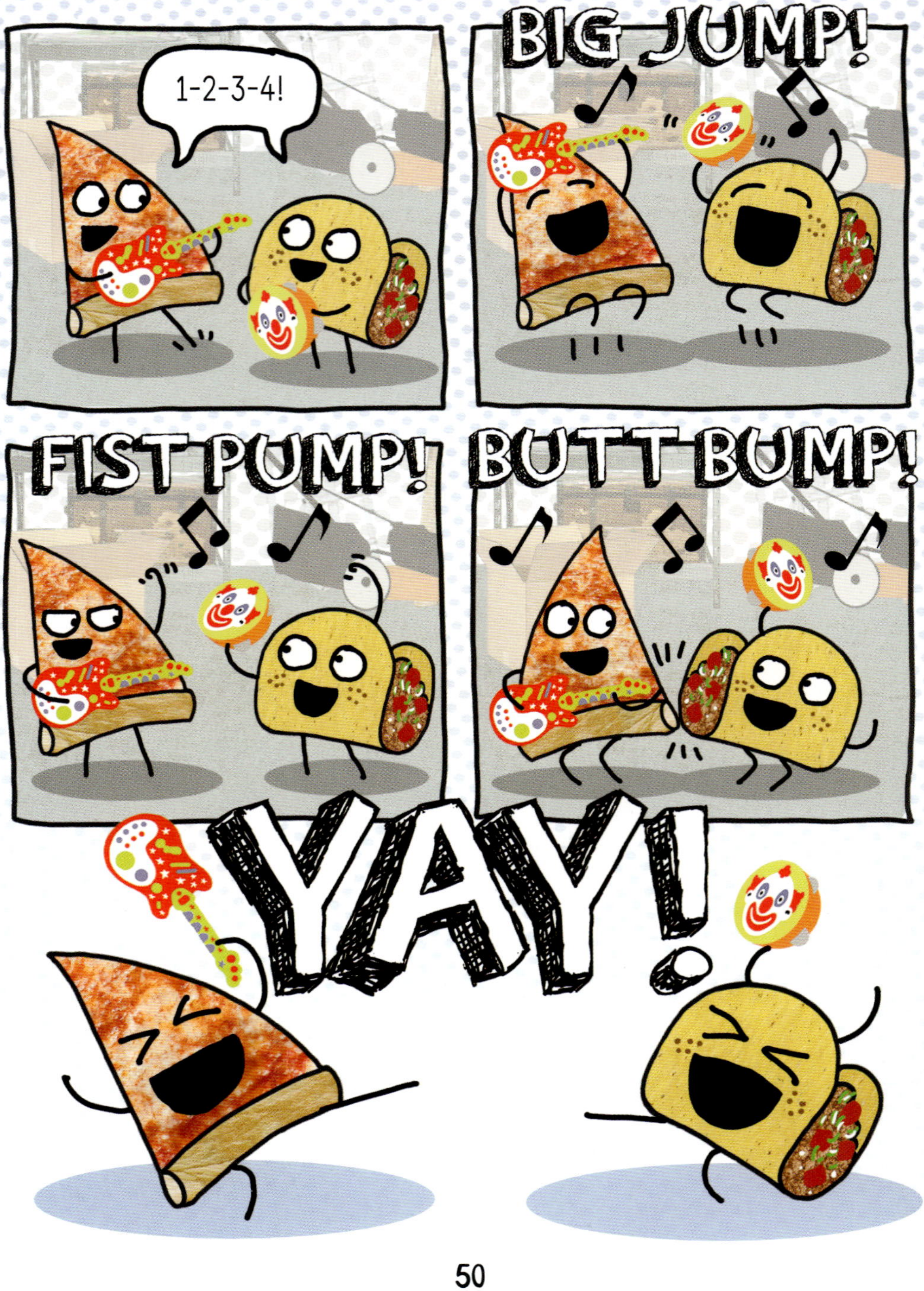
1-2-3-4!
BIG JUMP!
FIST PUMP!
BUTT BUMP!
YAY!

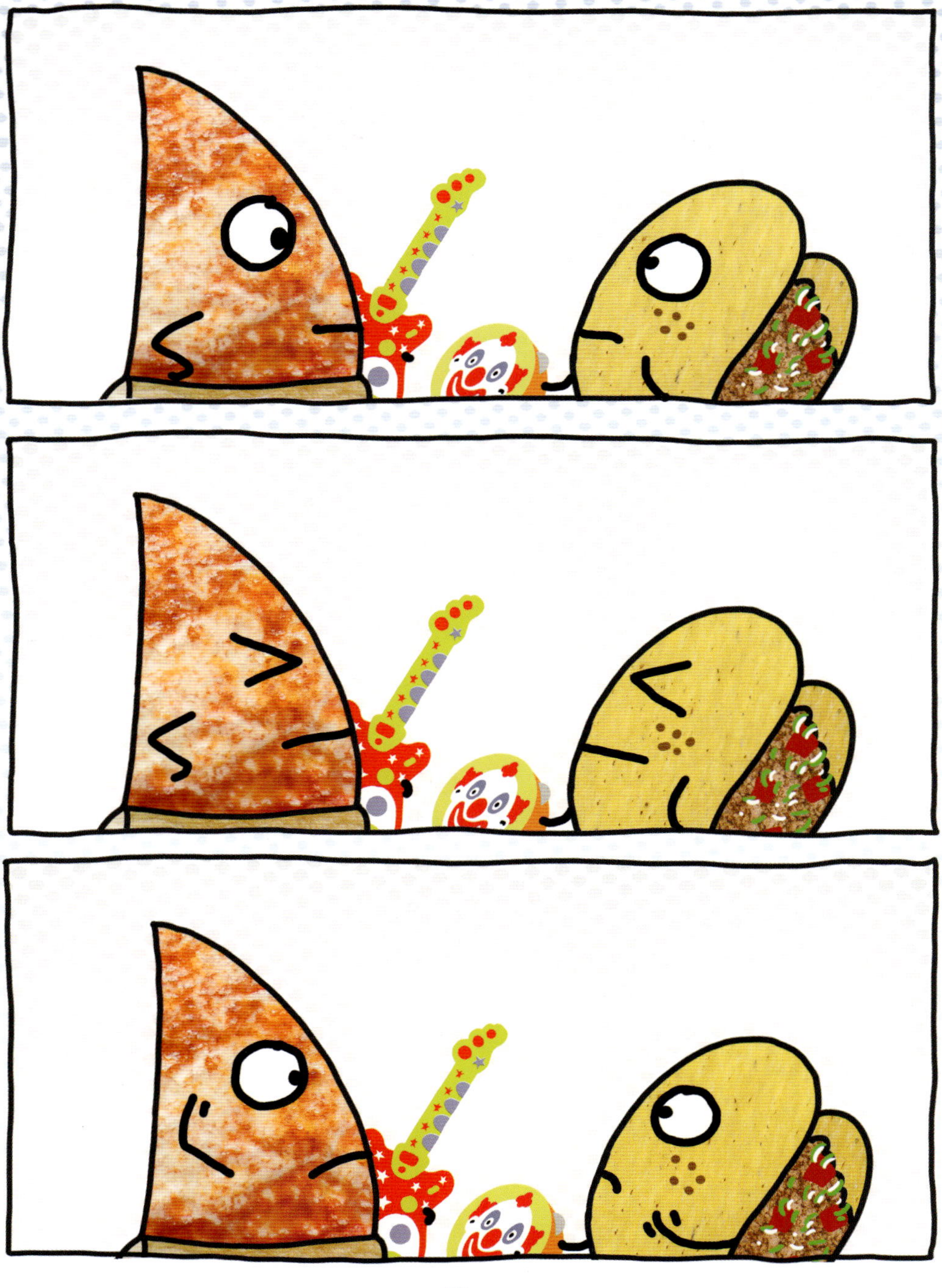

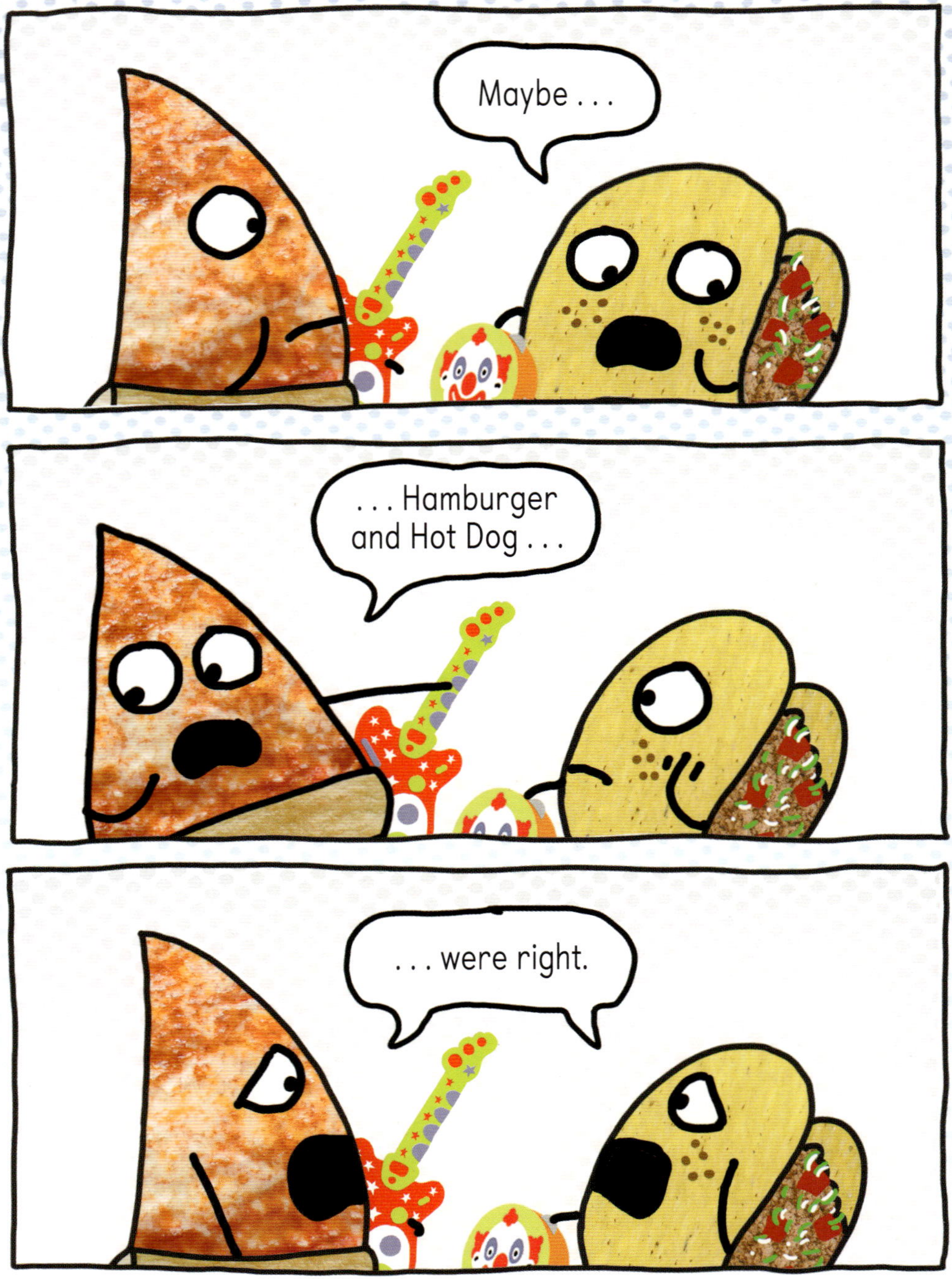
Maybe . . .
. . . Hamburger and Hot Dog . . .
. . . were right.

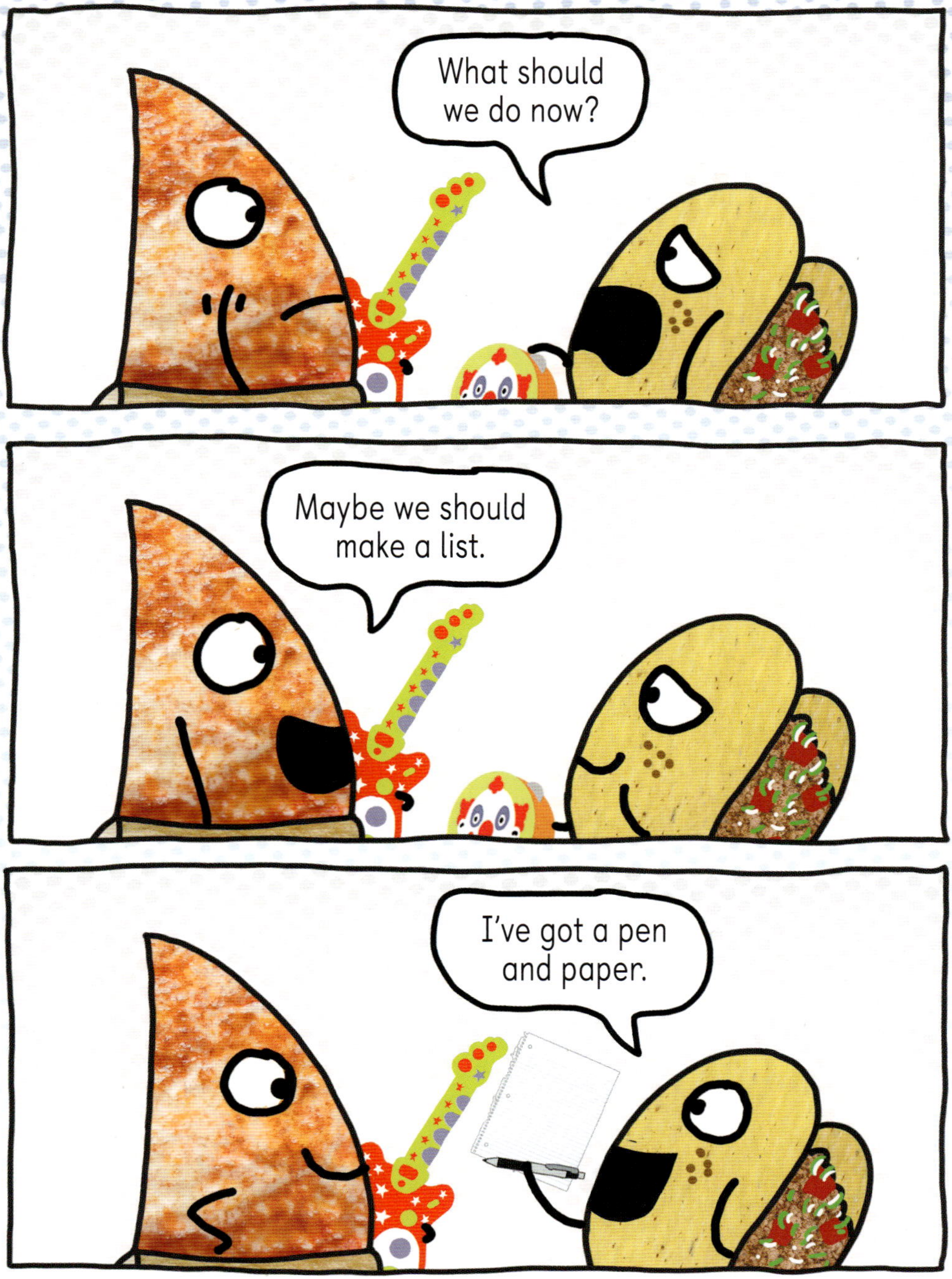
What should we do now?
Maybe we should make a list.
I’ve got a pen and paper.

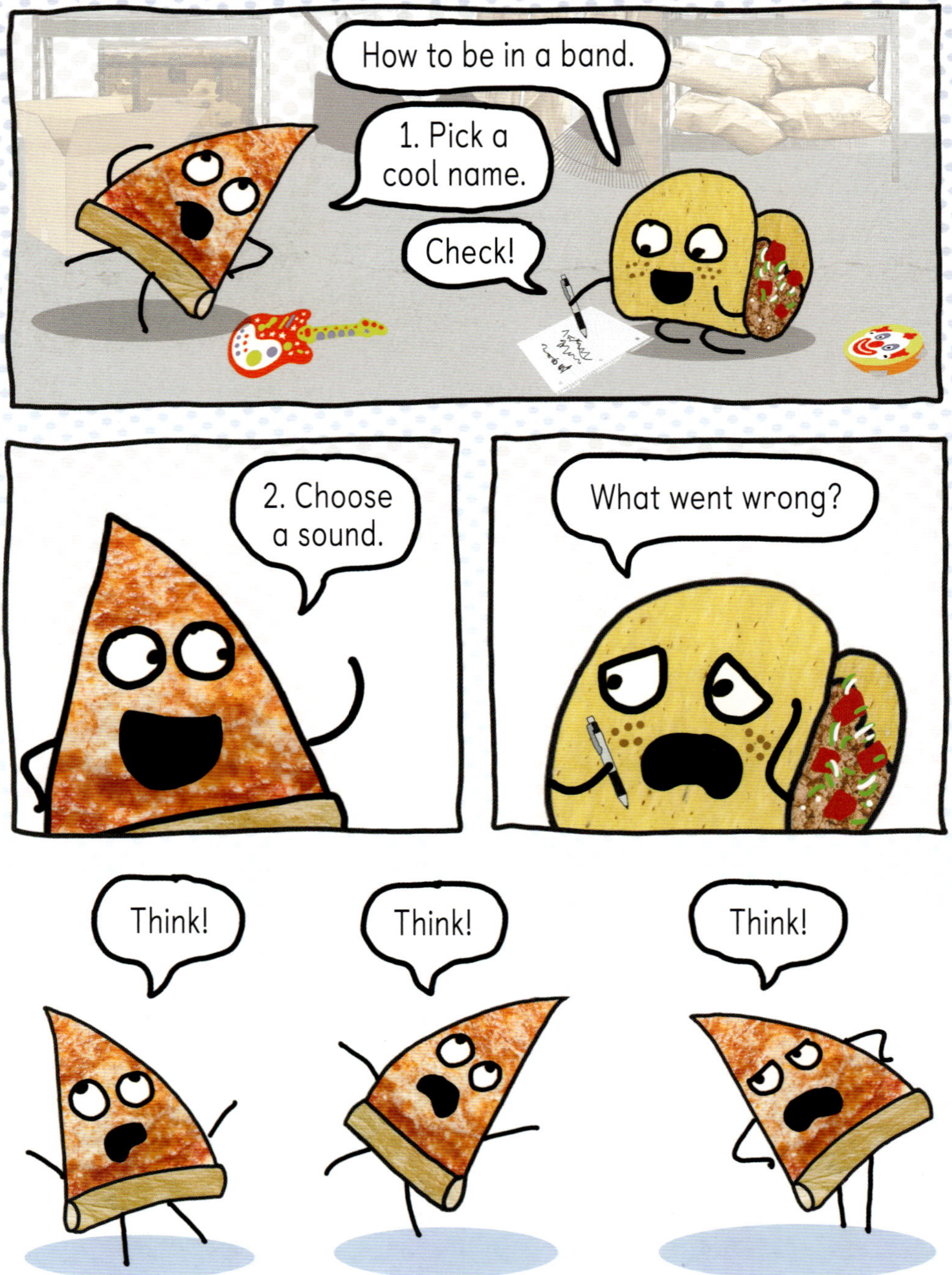
How to be in a band.
1. Pick a cool name.
Check!
2. Choose a sound.
What went wrong?
Think!
Think!
Think!

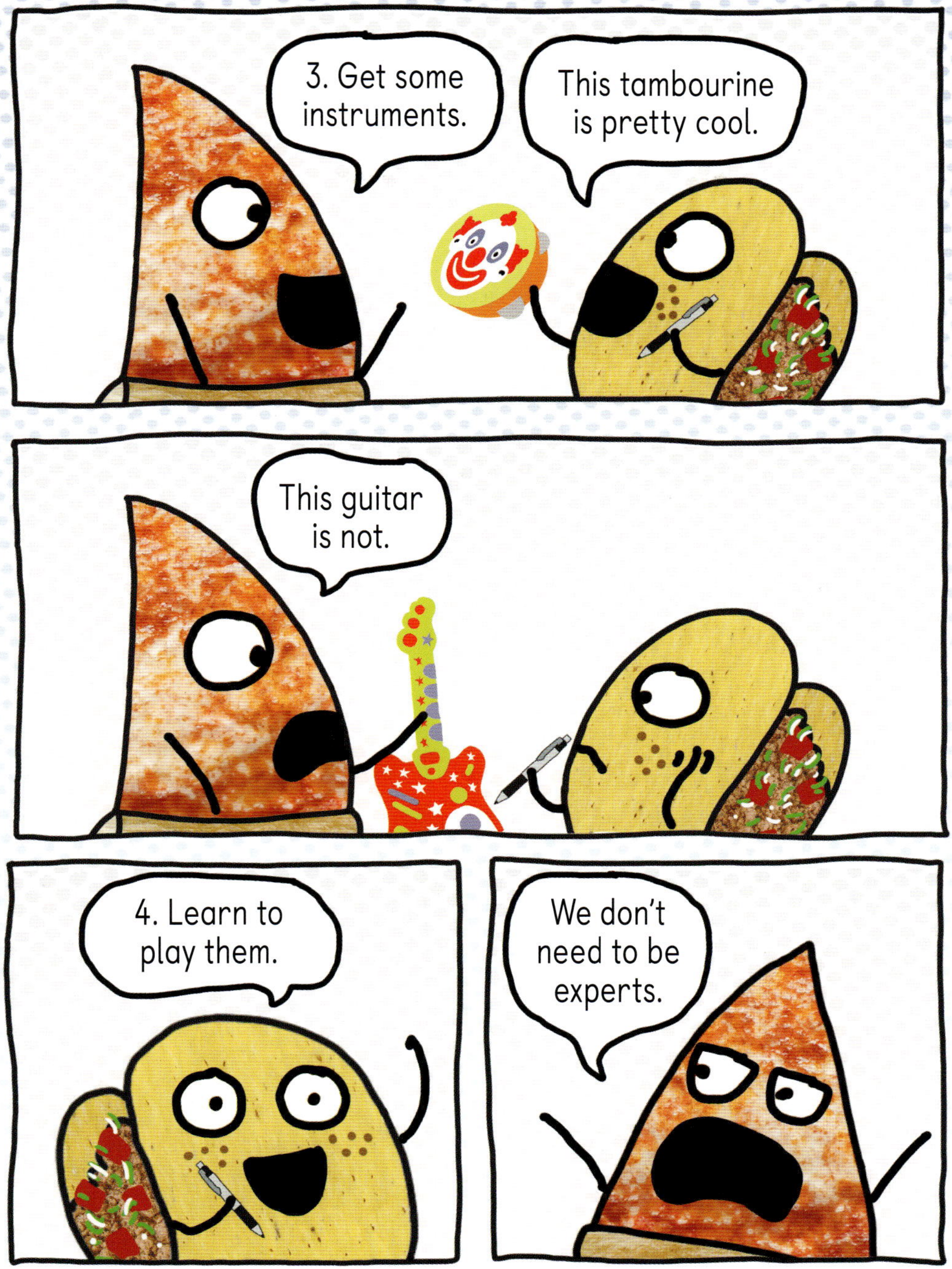
3. Get some instruments.
This tambourine is pretty cool.
This guitar is not.
4. Learn to play them.
We don't need to be experts.

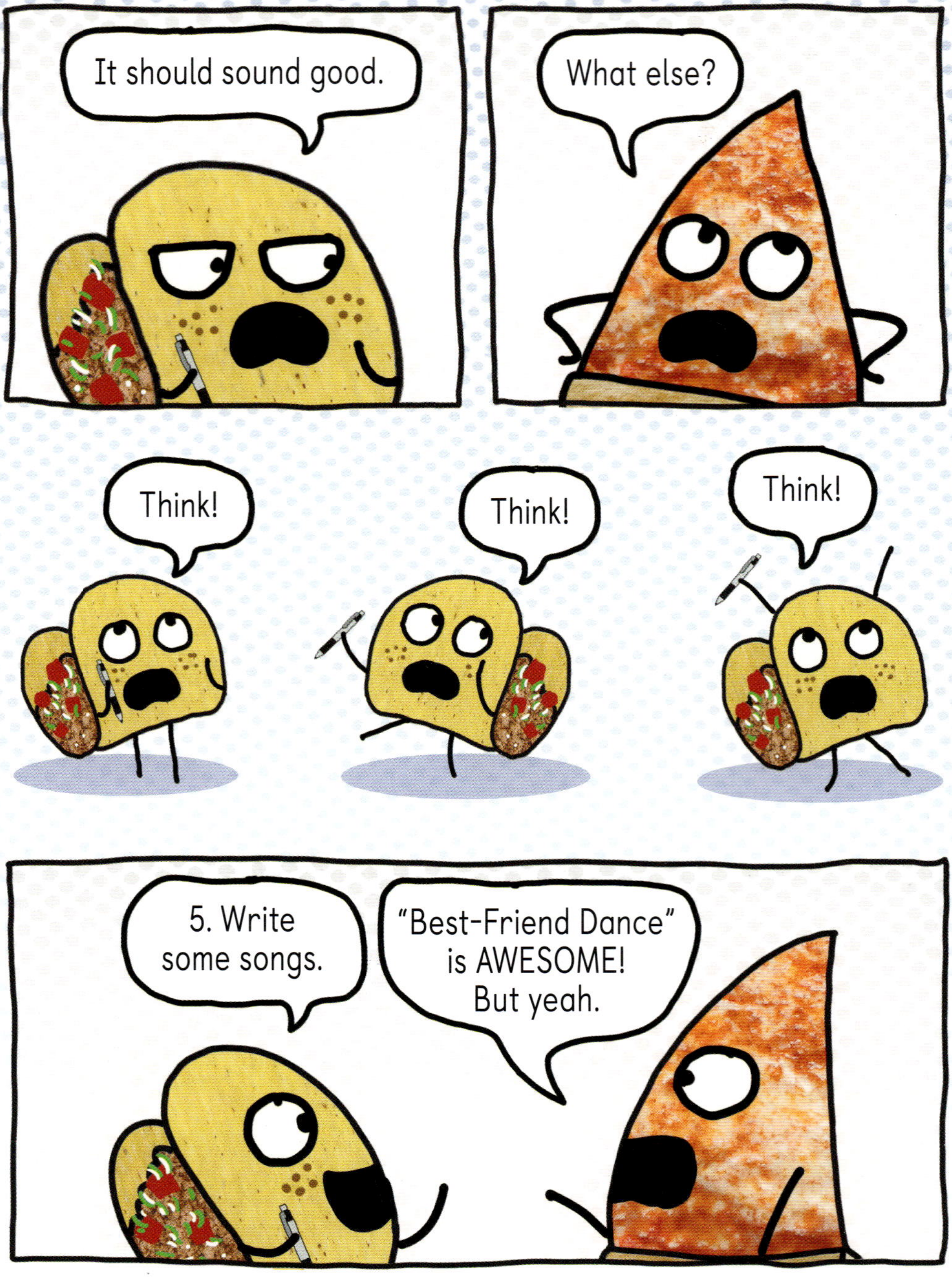
It should sound good.
What else?
Think!
Think!
Think!
5. Write some songs.
"Best-Friend Dance" is AWESOME! But yeah.

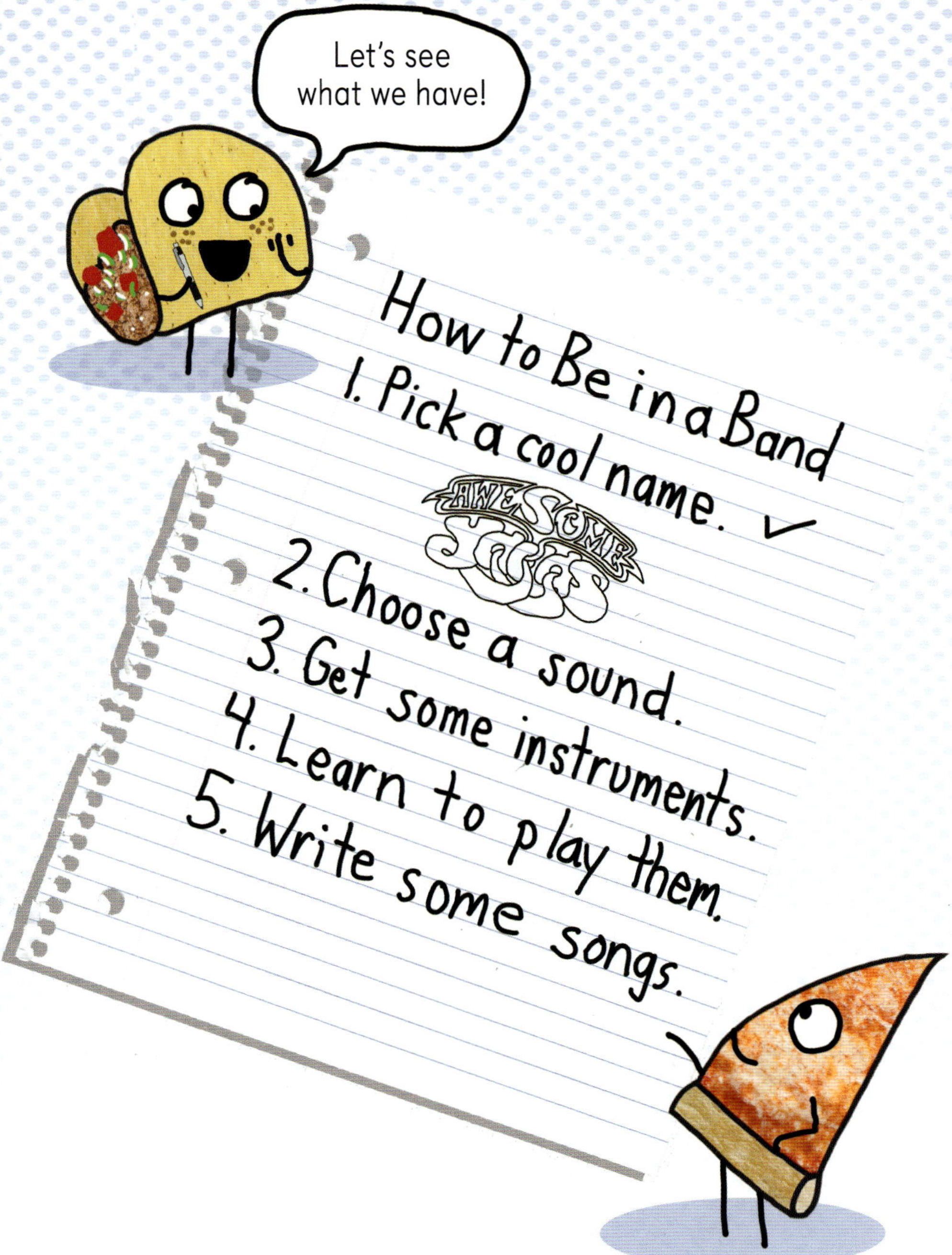
Let's see what we have!
How to Be in a Band
1. Pick a cool name. ✓
AWESOME
2. Choose a sound.
3. Get some instruments.
4. Learn to play them.
5. Write some songs.

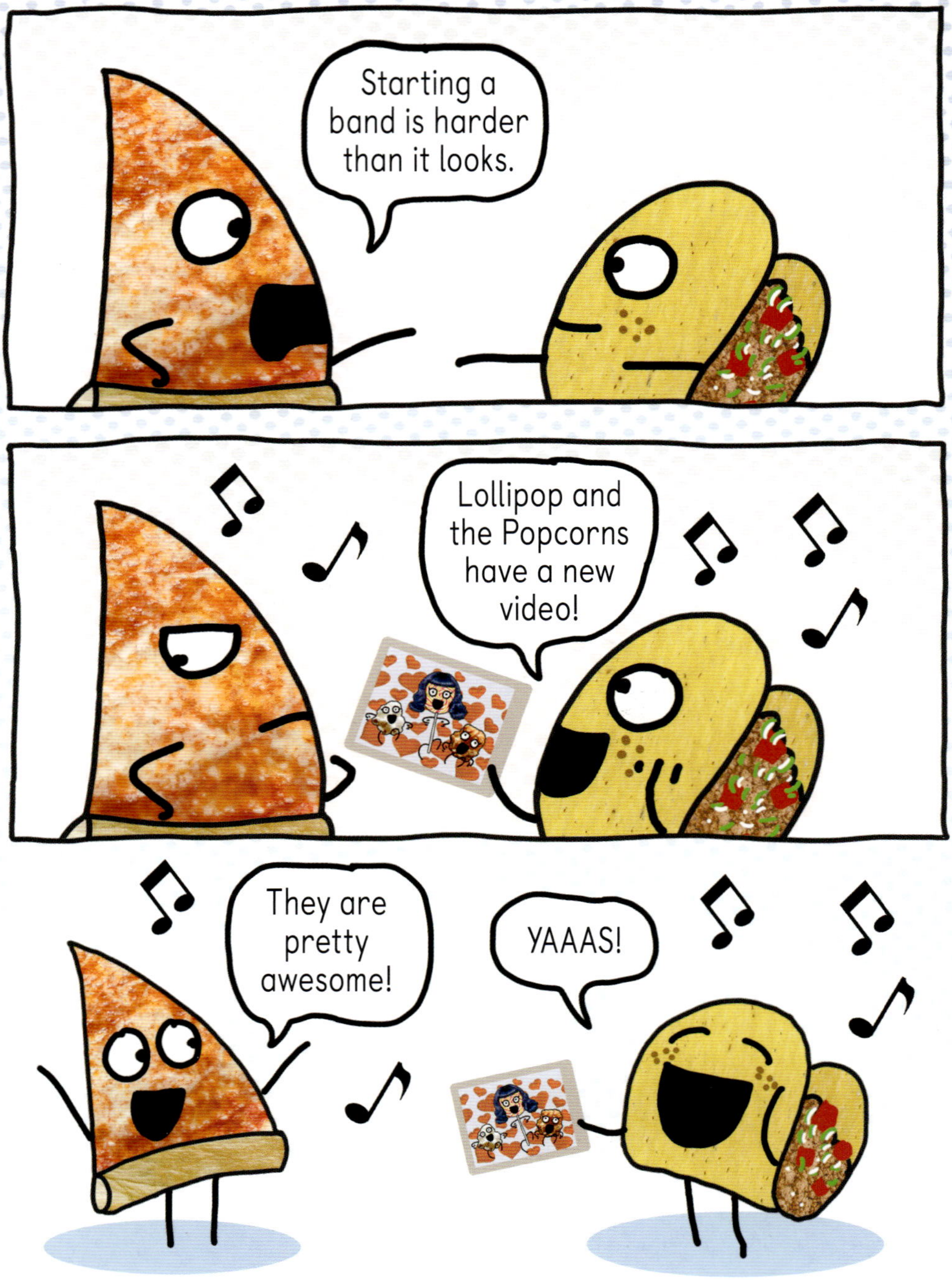

Starting a band is harder than it looks.
Lollipop and the Popcorns have a new video!
They are pretty awesome!
YAAAS!

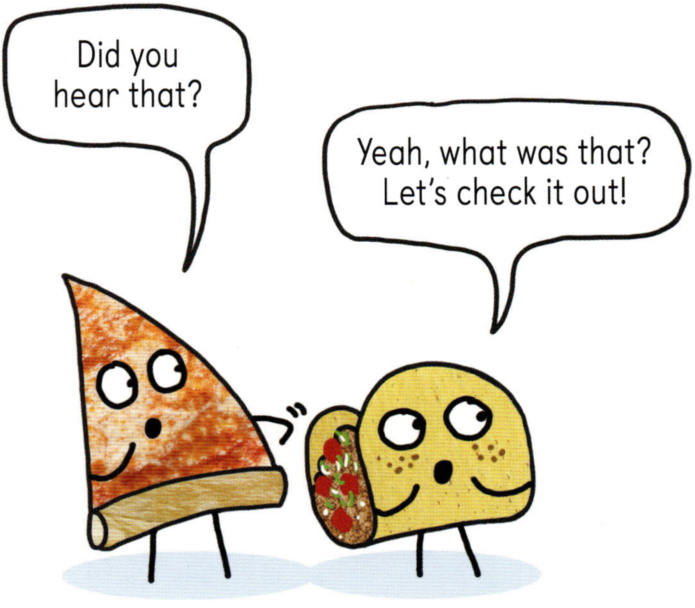
Did you hear that?
Yeah, what was that? Let's check it out!

PREPARE TO BE SCARED . . . IF YOU DARE!!

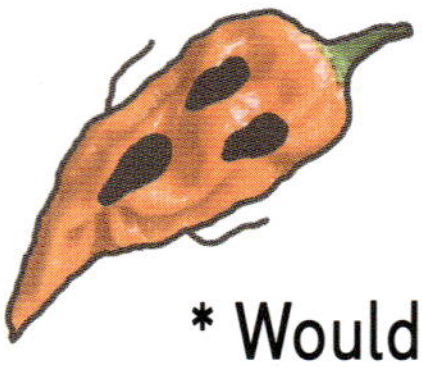

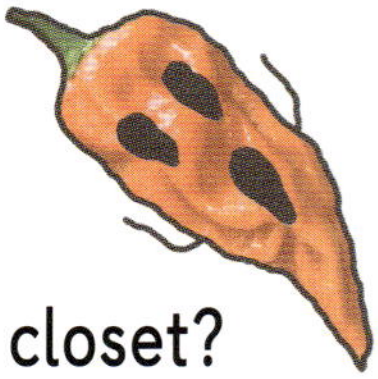

* Would you spend ten minutes alone in a dark closet?

* How about a dark basement?

* What's scarier than watching the scariest scary movie?

You'll see. . . . MWAH ha ha HA HA HA!!

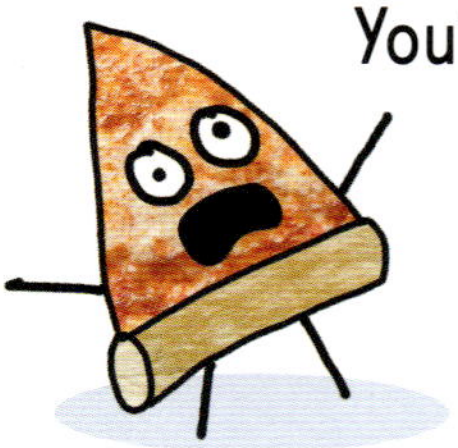

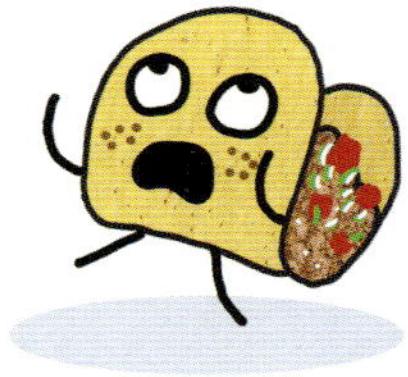

PIZZA AND TACO: DARE TO BE SCARED!

Coming in July 2023!

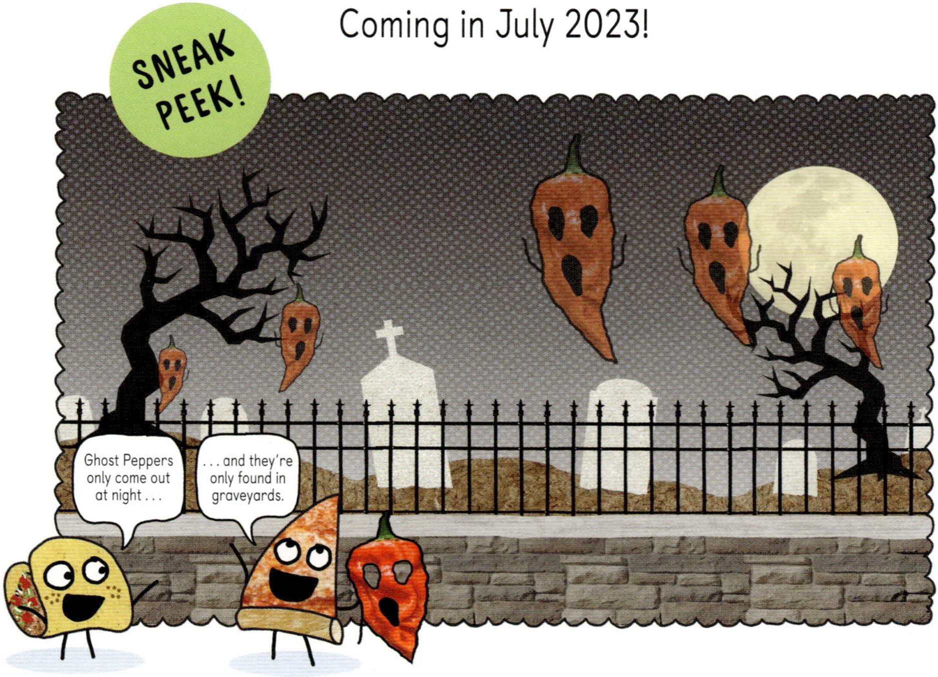
SNEAK PEEK!
Ghost Peppers only come out at night . . .
. . . and they're only found in graveyards.

AWESOME COMICS!
AWESOME KIDS!

Pizza and Taco
WHO'S THE BEST?
STEPHEN SHASKAN
Pizza and Taco
BEST PARTY EVER!
STEPHEN SHASKAN
Pizza and Taco
SUPER-AWESOME COMIC!
STEPHEN SHASKAN
Mika Song
DONUT FEED THE SQUIRRELS
Mika Song
APPLE OF MY PIE
MARY POPE OSBORNE'S
MAGIC TREE HOUSE
THE GRAPHIC NOVEL
DINOSAURS BEFORE DARK
ADAPTED BY JENNY LAIRD
ILLUSTRATED BY KELLY & NICHOLE MATTHEWS
MARY POPE OSBORNE'S
MAGIC TREE HOUSE
THE GRAPHIC NOVEL
THE KNIGHT AT DAWN
ADAPTED BY JENNY LAIRD
ILLUSTRATED BY KELLY & NICHOLE MATTHEWS
Kaeti Vandorn
MONSTER friends
GRUMPY MONKEY
FRESHLY SQUEEZED
Suzanne Lang
Max Lang
SCAREDY'S NUTTY ADVENTURES
Scaredy Squirrel
In a Nutshell
MELANIE WATT

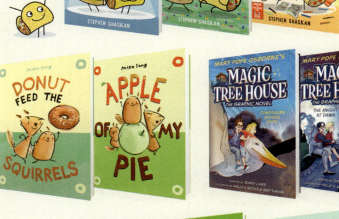

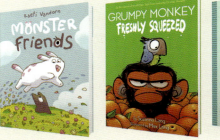